The Big Game

Jake head-faked to the left. I paid no attention to his head. The ball, I told myself, the ball. Just watch the ball. Then Jake began to work his way to the right from the top of the key. He dribbled the ball forward, but I wouldn't let him through to the hoop. I was on him, and I could tell that he was starting to get rattled because his eyes were darting back and forth. I think Jake was just too proud to pass the ball off, so he jumped, lofting it over my head, toward the basket.

He totally overshot, and that was just the chance I needed. As the ball teetered off the edge of the hoop, I grabbed it and sped down the court like lightning. Jake was the only one after me, but by the time I crossed the center line, I was alone. This was it! My chance! I sped on to the basket.

Books by Alison Jackson

Crane's Rebound
My Brother the Star

Available from MINSTREL Books

ALISON JACKSON

PUBLISHED BY POCKET BOOKS

New York   London   Toronto   Sydney   Tokyo   Singapore

This book is a work of fiction. Names, characters, places, and incidents are either products of the author's imagination or are used fictitiously. Any resemblance to actual events or locales or persons, living or dead, is entirely coincidental.

A Minstrel Book published by
POCKET BOOKS, a division of Simon & Schuster Inc.
1230 Avenue of the Americas, New York, NY 10020

Text copyright © 1991 by Alison Jackson

Illustrations copyright © 1991 by Diane Dawson Hearn

Published by arrangement with Dutton Children's Books

ISBN: 0-671-75878-0

First Minstrel Books printing August 1993

10 9 8 7 6 5 4 3 2

A MINSTREL BOOK and colophon are registered trademarks
of Simon & Schuster Inc.

Cover art by Daniel Horne

Printed in the U.S.A.

This one is for all my friends
at the Fullerton Public Library.

A. J.

With thanks to Lucia

D.D.H.

1

"I want to have a baby," my six-year-old brother announced one morning at the breakfast table.

Mom's reaction was fairly predictable. She screamed and dropped a cantaloupe on the floor.

"Cameron Crane!" she exclaimed. "Whatever could have put such an idea into your head?"

That was easy. If Mom had been paying any attention lately, she would have noticed Cam following me to my best friend Mike's house whenever he spied me sneaking out the front door. Mike's family had adopted a new baby just two months ago, and for some reason Cam was drawn to that little infant like a pig to mud.

Mostly, Cam would just sit and observe the baby in silence. But sometimes he would ask Mike's mom a question like "How come Kevin's fingers don't work right?" or "Why is he eating his foot?" If you ask me, he was a little obsessed.

I was about to explain my brother's new obsession to Mom, but Cam beat me to it.

"Mike's got a new baby brother," he informed her. "Why can't we have one too?"

Mom pressed her lips together and squeezed the retrieved cantaloupe between both palms, clearly at a loss for words.

I was enjoying this.

Cam continued. "Can't we just buy a new baby, like Mike's parents did?"

"Oh, dear." Mom sighed. Then she smiled kindly at him. "They didn't exactly pick Kevin off the shelf at Babies 'Я' Us, Cam. I think maybe someone should have a little talk with you." She shot a glance in my direction, but I threw my hands up in the air.

"Don't look at me!" I said. "We don't study that stuff until next year." Mike and I had just graduated from the fifth grade one month ago. Rumor had it that in Jefferson Middle School next fall, our life-science class was going to be very interesting.

Mom gave me a dirty look and turned back to Cam. "Well, why don't you go ask your father?" she suggested.

Cam put down his spoon and solemnly slid off

2

the chair. When his back was turned, Mom rolled her eyes at me.

"Buy a baby," she muttered, loud enough for me to hear. "As if the two of you aren't expensive enough!"

Mom started to clear the table as I leafed through the sports section of the newspaper. I really enjoyed all kinds of sports, but basketball was my special passion. In fact, I had been chosen to attend the county sports camp for junior-high-school kids this summer, and I would be leaving tomorrow. I was going to live for two weeks in the dorms at State College, playing basketball every minute of every day. I could hardly wait!

It made me a little jittery, though, thinking about playing ball with a bunch of seventh and eighth graders, especially when I had only just finished fifth grade myself. But I knew I was pretty good. After all, only two students had been chosen out of all the fifth graders in our county—and I was one of them.

To tell the truth, all that tryout business had been pretty scary at the time. We went through two sets of play-offs—in front of a big panel of judges—and the whole thing took about six weeks before the teams were finally chosen.

To make matters worse, I came down with the chicken pox in the middle of it all. And the only good thing about *that* was the fact that Cam caught them right after I did.

Just then Cam shuffled back into the kitchen, looking distressed. My father stepped through the door directly behind him. Dad was a good talker, being a car salesman and all. He could sell anything to almost anyone, but right now I don't think Cam was willing to buy this "baby" stuff.

Of course, I had already pretty much figured out what Cam's reaction would be. Once he found out that there had to be a girl involved, he wouldn't want any part of it.

"Darn!" Cam muttered, slapping his hand down on the table. "Why do girls always have to mess everything up?"

For once, I agreed with my little brother completely!

I guess maybe I forgot to mention that the other fifth grader chosen for the sports camp this summer was a girl. Jeez! Her name was Bobby Lorimer, and, unfortunately, her name got switched around with mine at the tryouts.

You see, my name is Leslie Crane. So I guess it's natural that some people might think I'm a girl. Before they get a good look at me, that is. I'm tall, skinny as a mop handle, and I look about as much like a girl as the Jolly Green Giant.

Not that I'm complaining. I mean, being tall has its advantages, especially when it comes to playing basketball. And I'm really a fanatic about that. I practice just about every day, and when I'm not practicing I'm making moves in my head.

Even though Mike is almost as big a basketball nut as I am, he told me that it's not normal to concentrate so hard on only one thing like that. But I think he was just being Mr. Sour Grapes, because he didn't get chosen to go to camp himself.

I considered two weeks of playing basketball without my best friend and immediately felt very sorry for myself. After all, Mike and I had played ball together ever since the third grade. Hardly a day went by that we didn't shoot hoops at his house or mine. So, why couldn't it have been Mike at State College with me for two weeks—instead of Bobby Lorimer? She always made me nervous.

The phone rang, and I put the newspaper down to answer it.

"Les?" It was Mike.

"Hi," I answered.

"Can you come over for a little one-on-one? I mean . . . since it's your last day at home and all?"

"Sure," I told him. "It sounds great! As long as I can sneak out without Cam following me. You know how he loves to fuss over that baby."

"Oh, yeah." Mike paused. "About the baby . . .

5

we might have to baby-sit him. But just for a little while.''

Wonderful! NOTHING interested me less than trying to shoot a few baskets with a dumb old baby hanging around.

"And we might even have to change his diaper," Mike added.

Well, almost nothing.

2

I left for Mike's house right away. And I was in luck. Cam had grudgingly agreed to go next door and play with Susie Walker, so I didn't even have to sneak out the back door this time.

Susie is a little girl who visits her grandmother every summer for a few weeks. Unfortunately, her grandmother happens to be our neighbor. Whenever Susie is there, she insists on dressing up their tired old basset hound and taking it for a walk. The only problem is that the dog is so old it probably hasn't intentionally walked anywhere in five years!

That doesn't stop Susie. She just drags the poor dog along the pavement on its belly. I'm not kidding! The dog follows behind her like a wagon without any wheels.

One day I actually stopped one of these

"walks" to ask Susie if the dog was still alive. Susie broke into tears and ran all the way back to her grandmother's front porch, leaving me to drag the dog the rest of the way home.

Now, as I was walking to Mike's house, I waved to Susie and Cam playing together in Mrs. Whittaker's front yard. Cam was grimly pushing the dog around the lawn in a baby carriage. He didn't even wave back.

When I got to Mike's house I found him practicing lay-up shots. The baby was lying in the middle of a blanket near the edge of the driveway.

I eyed Kevin warily. "Isn't that kind of dangerous?" I asked Mike.

"Naaah," he told me.

I dribbled the ball a few times and then sent it spiraling toward the hoop. It bounced off the edge and landed about six inches from Kevin's head.

"I can't shoot with that baby lying there!" I shouted.

Mike just laughed and retrieved the ball. "I know," he answered craftily. "What about Mom's car?"

"Huh?"

"She's gone anyway. We'll just put Kevin in the car seat, and he can watch us play from inside."

I shrugged. Why not?

Mike picked Kevin up and carried him over to

8

the car. Then I watched as he struggled with about five different safety straps. When he finally had the baby all buckled in, Mike slammed the door shut and grinned at me over the hood of the car.

"A captive audience," he said, wiggling his eyebrows up and down.

But then Kevin started wailing. I glared at him through the car window, and then I heard Mike muttering on the other side of the car.

"What's wrong?" I asked as he raced past me and jiggled the door handle on my side.

"Oh, no," he said, and leaned helplessly against the door. "I locked the baby in the car!"

My first instinct was to laugh, but I didn't think that would be too smart. Or too nice.

"Don't you have a spare set of keys?" I asked him.

"Probably, but I don't know where they are." Mike was making faces at the baby. Kevin smiled back and drooled.

"Where is your dad?" I asked Mike. "Doesn't he have some keys to your mom's car?"

"He had to go in to work for a few hours this morning."

"Oh," I sighed.

Kevin started crying again. Mike tapped on the window and stuck out his tongue until Kevin plugged up his mouth with his thumb.

Mike frowned. "I'll have to run inside and call Dad," he said. Mike took off in a sprint, up the steps and into his house.

Kevin started whimpering then. I bugged my eyes out at him and stuck my fingers in my ears. The whimpers turned into howls. I pressed both palms against the window as hard as I could and began shaking the car back and forth. Kevin smiled, so I pushed harder. He laughed, and I laughed back at him.

But then I looked over the top of the car and the laughter got stuck in my throat. Two kids were pedaling down the street on bicycles. They were only three houses away, and one of them was Bobby Lorimer! The other was Tim Lorimer, her older brother. He was a terrific ball player and had also been selected for our sports camp this summer. I really liked him. Well, to be honest, I envied him.

Bobby I wasn't so sure about. But I couldn't let either one of them see me baby-sitting a child who was locked up inside a Volvo. Talk about looking stupid! So I did the first thing that came to me. I slid under the car on my stomach.

"Hey, look! A little kid is in that car, and he's screaming!" I recognized Bobby's voice. I could picture her crinkling her nose up the way she did when she was thinking real hard or concentrating

11

on a difficult shot. In fact, she was probably doing some pretty heavy nose crinkling right this minute.

Then two pairs of shoes stopped right in front of my face: Tim's Nikes and a smaller pair of dirty white sneakers with bright orange laces that had to be Bobby's.

Someone tried the door. "It's locked!" exclaimed Bobby. "Do you think we should call the police?"

"No," I heard Tim answer. "I'm sure that the kid's mom just ran into the house for something."

The dirty sneakers began prancing around on tiptoe, and I figured that Bobby was probably performing for the baby, to make him stop crying. It reminded me of the way she darted around the basketball court, constantly getting in my way.

The Nikes backed away from the car. "Come on, Bobby. We gotta go. Les wasn't at home anyway, and I told Mom we'd be back for lunch."

They had stopped at my house?

Even through the exhaust pipes and transmission I could hear Kevin cranking up again over my head. Tim and Bobby hurriedly climbed on their bikes and pedaled away. When they wheeled around the corner, I crawled out from under the car. My sweatshirt was covered with grease, and my hands were black.

Mike ran up to me and stopped. "What happened to you?" he demanded.

"Ummm. The ball rolled under the car."

Mike just shook his head and stared at me as if I had completely lost my mind. "Dad will be here in five minutes," he informed me. Then he got this goofy grin on his face, and I just knew what he was going to say next.

"Hey, wasn't that Bobby Lorimer I saw riding by?" Mike asked with a wink. He was always giving me trouble about Bobby, but I secretly thought he might be just a little bit jealous because she was picked over him for the sports camp.

"Uhhh. Yeah," I admitted.

"Ooooh-laaaa-laaaa!" Mike sang in a horrible French accent. Then he began to make kissing noises. I was not amused.

Kevin was, though. He started giggling and cooing at us from the backseat of the car. That made Mike laugh even harder.

I scowled at them. What had Bobby and Tim wanted with me anyway? It was a long bike ride across town for the two of them.

I wasn't about to admit this to Mike, but I sort of wished I had been at home when they knocked on my door, instead of here playing one-on-one with my best friend and an imprisoned baby.

3

That night at dinner—my last night at home for two weeks—we were all a little sad. All of us except Cam, that is. He was already on his third ear of corn, butter dripping down his chin onto the tablecloth.

"I'm really going to miss you while you're away at camp, Les," my mom said. Her eyes were all scrunched up, and she had a sad sort of half-smile on her face.

"I will too," Dad added.

Cam was silent.

"What time will the bus be picking you up tomorrow?" Dad asked me.

"Seven-thirty in the morning," I answered, rolling my eyes. "That means I'll probably have to set my alarm—"

Cam started choking on his corn, and we all stopped to look at him. "I-I think I just lost my first tooth," he said. Cam opened his mouth real wide to show us some half-chewed corn kernels and a gap in his upper jaw.

Normally, Cam's interruptions made me mad enough to spit, but tonight I was so excited about sports camp that this one only irritated me a little. So I just sneered across the table after Cam made his announcement.

"Oh, Cam! Your first tooth! How exciting! Where is it?" My mom always got a little over-dramatic about things like this. My own first tooth was wrapped up in a box somewhere with my first burp rag.

"Well . . . umm . . . I think that maybe I might have swallowed it," Cam answered slowly.

"You think that you swallowed your tooth?" Dad exclaimed. "How do you expect to collect from the tooth fairy?"

"Oh, come on, Dad! I don't believe in that stuff!" said Cam.

"Then I guess you don't believe in getting a dollar either," I grumbled at him.

"A dollar!" Dad said. "I seem to remember a quarter a few years ago."

"It was a dime in my day," Mom added, as she spooned out some mashed potatoes.

"Hey wait, Mom. This is the nineties," I said. Then I stabbed a piece of meat with my fork and waved it at her. "It's called *the law of supply and demand.*"

"I can't see much demand for a tooth that's down in Cam's gut," my father said jokingly. He winked at Mom.

"Dad!" Cam squealed.

"Okay, Cam. A dollar it is."

"No fair!" I shouted. "I only got quarters for mine."

"Hey, Les. This is the nineties," Dad reminded me with a chuckle. "A quarter was worth more five years ago. It's called *inflation.*"

"Then, if I were you, Cam," I said slowly, "I'd save the next tooth until you're at least eighteen." By my figuring, his tooth would be worth over a hundred bucks by then.

Cam seemed to consider this for a minute. Then he surprised us all.

"You know, Dad," Cam began, turning to look at my father intently, "I thought about what you told me this morning . . . about babies and all. Would it cost anything for Susie and me to *borrow* a baby? Just for a little while?"

"Not babies again!" Dad sighed and rubbed a hand over his bald spot.

Mom giggled and began clearing the table.

"Oh, so you and Susie are getting pretty serious, huh?"

"Well, Susie's all right," Cam said. "Only she makes me burp her dolls. Which is stupid, because they don't even eat anything." He wiped his greasy chin with a napkin and got up to leave the table.

"Be thankful they don't!" Dad called out after him, and we both started laughing.

Cam and I shared a bedroom, so things got pretty touchy sometimes. After dinner I caught him going through my desk for the hundredth time, so I constructed a barricade across the room while he took his bath. My barricade was made of shoes—every pair of shoes I owned, lined up heel to toe—and it was really a masterpiece of engineering.

Mom didn't agree. She stopped right behind me and tapped me on the shoulder.

"You can put those shoes away, right after I stash this dollar under Cam's pillow."

"But he doesn't even have a tooth to show for it," I grumbled. I was miffed at her. Mom could have at least praised my workmanship.

"There's a hole in his mouth," she answered. "That's good enough for me." My mother took the dollar and tucked it under Cam's yellow pillow. Then she settled herself down on the end of his bed while I put my shoes in the closet.

"I was only establishing my territorial boundaries," I mumbled crossly. "Like dogs do."

Mom made a face, and I had to laugh.

"Well . . . not EXACTLY like dogs do," I admitted.

When I had the last shoe in place I sat down beside her on Cam's bed and she put an arm around me.

"I really am going to miss you, Les," she said. "You've never been away from home for two whole weeks before."

I swallowed a tiny lump in my throat and just nodded at her. I figured she was waiting for me to say I was going to miss her too.

But I couldn't. The truth was I was too afraid to say anything. Because if I did, I might start blubbering or something, just like a little kid leaving to spend the night at a friend's house for the first time.

I was going to miss her a lot. I think Mom knew it. And I was pretty nervous about camp too. Well, that's not exactly right. I was actually terrified. Playing basketball was the one real thing I was good at, but what if all those big guys in junior high were a thousand times better than I was? I mean, I did want to learn something at camp, but I didn't want to look like a fool doing it.

Mom gave my shoulder a little squeeze, and I patted her hand awkwardly. Then I turned my face up to hers and made a funny face, crossing my eyes at her.

"Oh, you!" Mom laughed. She threw Cam's pillow at me, and the dollar bill fluttered into the air, doing a couple of somersaults. We had to catch Cam's tooth money in midair and hide it all over again.

4

Dad dropped me off in the parking lot of Jefferson Middle School at a quarter to seven the next morning.

"Good luck," he said, holding a thumb up out the car window.

I fidgeted with the strap of my duffel bag. "Thanks, Dad," I said, swallowing hard.

As I watched Dad's car pull away, I actually considered running after him. I mean, after all, I was the only one here, as far as I could tell. The bus wasn't even here yet, for crying out loud! I started to panic. What if the whole thing had been a mistake? What if the entire sports camp had been canceled? And I was the only kid who didn't know about it?

Some cars pulled into the lot and I began to breathe a little easier. Then I knew I was in the right place, because I heard someone shout "Hey, Ichabod!" across the nearly empty parking lot.

Jeez! It was Bobby Lorimer. She was climbing out of a blue van and heading my way. Just because I was skinny and my last name was Crane, some of the kids at my school called me Ichabod, after that goofy guy in "The Legend of Sleepy Hollow," but did Bobby have to repeat that dumb nickname of mine?

A few more cars drove into the school parking lot. Trunks were slamming shut and kids were yelling good-bye to their parents. I figured that if I just ignored Bobby, no one else would even have to know that "Ichabod" was really me.

That didn't work. Bobby ran up to me and plopped her bag down on the pavement, right next to mine. Then she crinkled up her nose in that special way that always got me flustered and sort of dizzy.

"Tim and I stopped by your house yesterday to ask if maybe you wanted to go see a movie with us," Bobby said.

Go see a movie? With a girl? With Bobby Lorimer? This made me feel excited and frightened at the same time.

"Oh," I replied, trying to act real casual. "What movie was it?"

"*The Return of Zorg!*"

I stared blankly at her.

21

"It's about this monster that has two heads—"

"Wait a minute!" I interrupted. "*The RETURN of Zorg*? I never saw him when he came around the first time."

"That doesn't matter. He killed everyone in the first movie anyway."

"So who's left to kill?"

"I don't know. That's why I wanted to go see the second one."

See what I mean about Bobby? She could be really weird sometimes.

A very tall girl with straight brown hair ran up to us and threw her bag down too. It landed right on top of mine.

"Hi, Bobby," the girl shouted. She gave Bobby a good-natured thump on the back, and Bobby smiled up at her. Then the tall girl lowered her gaze to me. It made me feel funny, and then I realized why. I'm not used to looking up at people because I'm so tall myself.

"Charlotte, this is Les," Bobby said, tugging on my sleeve. "Les, this is Charlotte Nass. She's a friend of my brother's, from school."

I was going to say "Hi," but Charlotte took care of that with a hearty thump on my back. I lurched forward, nearly tripping over her bag. My eyes began to water, and it took me a moment to catch my breath.

"How's it going, kid?" Charlotte said, helping me up. Then she stepped on my foot, and I let out a yelp.

"Oh. Umm. Sorry," said Charlotte, slowly lifting her foot from on top of mine.

I stared down at my foot. I didn't want to say anything to her. There aren't a lot of guys who will admit this, but girls who are taller than I am make me really nervous. They throw me off balance or something.

So I just looked up and gave Charlotte a thin smile. But she suddenly aimed a broad grin over the top of my head. "Hey, Janet! How's it going?" she hollered to someone else.

Charlotte took off across the parking lot to meet her friend, who was climbing the stairs of the bus. Then she ran back to grab her bag.

"See ya, Bobby," Charlotte yelled over one shoulder. "You too, kid!"

"Does she play basketball?" I asked, frowning at Bobby. There were going to be other sports at the camp besides basketball, and I hoped Charlotte Nass would be playing one of them. Let's face it: With competition like her, I might as well have gone home right then and there.

Bobby laughed. "No. Charlotte is a volleyball player. And she's pretty good too."

"I'll bet," I said, picking up my bag and head-

24

ing for the bus. Bobby climbed the steps right behind me.

I wanted a seat in the very back, as far away from Charlotte as possible. She smiled at Bobby and me as we passed by her. I didn't smile back.

I know that was kind of mean, but Charlotte bugged me. She was so loud, and I hate it when other kids call me kid!

I chose a window seat, and Bobby sat down right next to me, crinkling her nose at me again. My hands suddenly started to sweat, so I quickly rubbed my palms across the front of my T-shirt.

Bobby's brother Tim boarded the bus right behind Bobby. He walked up the center aisle and sat down in the empty seat right in front of us. After stashing his bag under the seat, he turned around to look at me.

"Hi, Leslie. What's up?"

I was just starting to answer him when a beefy-looking guy with a blond buzz cut sat down in the seat with Tim.

"LESLIE!" he howled. "What kind of a name is that for a guy?" He was really yukking it up, having a great time watching my face turn three different shades of pink.

"It's a British name!" Bobby answered for me, crinkling up her nose at him. Now, how did she know that?

Why didn't she just stay out of it anyway, I thought dismally. This was definitely one of those moments when I felt like killing her.

"British!" shrieked Buzz-Head, turning all the way around to get a better look at me. Then he doubled up over the back of his seat, the top of his fuzzy head almost touching my chest. I'm not kidding! He was laughing like a half-crazed axe murderer or something.

"Lay off, Jake," Tim said quietly. And Buzz-Head did, but he was still grinning at me. Then he turned to Tim. "Oh, come on, Lorimer." He laughed. "I was just joking."

Tim finally cracked a smile and looked back at me. "This is Jake Lambert," he informed me. I nodded at Tim, but I was too afraid to utter a word to the maniac. "Since our names both start with 'L,' our lockers are right next to each other at school," Tim added.

"Hey, sorry, little buddy," Jake muttered with a lopsided grin. "No hard feelings, okay?" He reached out a hand to give me the high five, and when he was through with that, my fingers were vibrating, clear up to the knuckles.

After Jake turned around again, I made a face at Bobby and she giggled. Then she leaned over and whispered to me, "Jake was at the camp last year. Tim says he was the best player there."

That figured, I thought to myself. I stared straight ahead, eyeing the back of Jake's head cautiously. What could be worse than having this guy at camp with us for two weeks, I wondered?

I found out two hours later.

Having Jake as a roommate was definitely worse.

Jake, Tim, and I were all squeezed into a dorm room hardly bigger than a bathroom.

"Hey, dig this!" Jake hooted. "We'll be cozier than three hot dogs in a bun!"

Tim laughed. I smiled grimly. The excitement of being chosen to room with Tim Lorimer had suddenly dimmed. I decided that three was really a crowd.

"How do they ever fit three big college guys in here?" Tim wondered.

Jake rolled his eyes. "Those college dudes never stay in their rooms anyway," he said, laughing loudly.

Jake started dribbling a basketball across the linoleum floor. Then he did a little dance, passing the ball between his legs. And I had to admit it: The guy was a pretty good ball-handler.

"Do you always bring your own ball with you?" I asked warily, veering around Jake and throwing myself down on one of the empty beds.

"Hey, man! This isn't just any ball. This ball has been blessed by the very hands of Magic Johnson himself!"

I sat up, impressed. There was a smudged autograph on the surface of Jake's ball. The name could have been Magic Johnson's, for all I could tell.

"I call it my MAGIC ball," Jake continued, "because when I take a shot with this ball, I never miss. Well . . . almost never."

I glanced over at Tim, but he was nodding slowly at me, in agreement.

"It's true," Tim said seriously. "He's the best."

I looked back at Jake. He grinned at me and gave the ball a spin on the tip of his finger. Was this guy for real? A magic ball? What next?

After lunch, we spent our first afternoon practicing drills. Coach White divided us into practice groups and explained some of the rules and procedures for the next two weeks. We would be drilling for the first few days. Then, if our shots were good enough, we could start in on some offensive and defensive plays, and eventually graduate to playing real games.

"If any of you is late for practice," the coach warned us, "you can stay an hour afterward and help polish the floors." When a few of the guys

28

groaned, Coach White lowered his eyes at them. "On your hands and knees," he added.

"With your wrists tied behind your back and the rag clenched between your teeth," whispered the guy next to me. His name was Joe Minelli, and I recognized him from the tryouts last spring.

I heard the redheaded boy behind me start laughing. "Joe's just kidding," he said, poking me in the back.

When I was teamed up with Joe and the redhead for our drills later, I found out that his name was Steve Crawford. The three of us practiced lay-ups and free throws together for over an hour. And I don't know about them, but by that time my arms ached, and my back was beginning to hurt too, right under the shoulder blades.

Dribble, dribble, shoot. Dribble, dribble, shoot. I wished we were playing a real game. Dribble, dribble, shoot. Dribble, dribble, shoot. It was like being hypnotized. Or walking in your sleep. Everything was so automatic.

Maybe that's why it took me so long to notice that Joe had stopped dribbling. He held the ball up to his chest and pointed over at Jake on the court next to us. Steve stopped to watch too. In fact, the two of them just sort of stood and stared at Jake like he was some kind of hero or something. Then I noticed that Bobby was watching

Jake from court number four. And I couldn't help it. I stared over at him too.

Dribble, dribble, shoot. Jake canned a perfect shot. Dribble, dribble, shoot. Another. And another. Could that ball really be magic?

I glanced over at Bobby and decided to try my shot again. Dribble, dribble, shoot. Darn! The ball teetered on the edge of the hoop and then fell short. I let my eyes roam over to Jake again. He was just grinning at me, his eyes half closed like a lizard's.

After practice and showers, everyone went to eat in the huge dorm cafeteria. I was exhausted, and I couldn't even remember what I shoveled into my mouth. The volleyball, soccer, and gymnastics teams all shared meals in the same cafeteria, and I had never been elbowed by so many athletes in my life. Not even in a rough game of all-out jungle ball!

I got back to my room and collapsed across the top of my bed in a heap, wondering why I had ever looked forward to these two weeks.

But before I could close my eyes, Jake poked his head through the doorway of our room.

"Hey, Crane!" he yelled. "Phone call. For YOU!"

"Thanks." I sat up and stumbled into the hall.

"This is Les," I said into the receiver.

"Hi, Les. It's Cam."

Cam! "You okay?" I asked him.

"Oh, yeah. Sure," he replied calmly. "I just needed some money."

Money? I had this scary feeling that my piggy bank was sitting on his lap right now—with a hammer over it.

"What for?" I asked him shakily.

"Well . . . Dad told me that kids can get pretty expensive, so I wanted to start saving up some money now."

Oh, for cryin' out loud! When was this going to stop?

"I was wondering if you could give me a raise for watching Max," Cam said. Max was my pet hamster. One month ago, Cam would have been thrilled to pieces to take care of him for free.

"A raise! I'm already giving you a dime a day. Plus one Monopoly dollar."

"Oh, come on, Les. I can get more than that for one lousy tooth!"

What had my parents created here? A tooth grubber?

"Then you can just yank out the rest of them, for all I care!" I replied.

I heard sniffling on the other end of the phone.

"Okay, Cam," I offered, caving in. "How about fifty cents a day?"

There was a long silence on the other end,

while I listened to Cam breathing. He couldn't have been multiplying in his head. My brother was too young to know his times tables yet.

"Make it a dollar a day, and it's a deal," Cam replied.

He had me, and I knew it. Who else was going to take care of Max if I refused?

"All right, but next time I'm taking Max over to Mike's house." I hung up the phone and made my way back to bed.

Not only was I going to be subjected to a hot-shot roommate, exhaustion, and boring drills for the next two weeks. I was also going to be paying my little brother thirteen dollars while I was doing it!

5

Before breakfast the following morning, the guys in our dorm had a meeting with our dorm captain. All eighteen of us were squeezed together in the dorm "living room," which was about as big as a normal-sized bedroom.

I had never seen so many tall guys scrunched into one room before. And I don't think the dorm captain had either. He was sitting on the floor, near the window, gazing up at us like a mouse lost in a clump of palm trees.

Our captain was a college student who got to have a room all to himself and was probably paid lots of money just to baby-sit us. His name was Waldo, and at the moment he was wearing a tie and black socks, even though it was the middle of summer.

"I know that Coach White is responsible for

you on the basketball courts," Waldo told us, shoving a couple of spiky curls away from his thick, black-rimmed glasses. "However, I am in charge of this hall and all of the participants in the basketball camp."

"What about Bobby?" Jake yelled across the room. He was sitting at the bottom of the stairs, with that big orange ball of his resting on top of one knee. A couple of the guys hooted, and Jake smiled at them.

"Who?" Waldo asked. His eyes were suddenly very big behind his glasses, as he checked the roll sheets spread out in front of him.

"Don't bother looking," Tim said quietly. "She's not in this dorm."

"*She?*" Waldo looked up.

"Bobby's my sister," Tim explained.

"And she's on the basketball team?" Waldo asked, squinting at him.

"Yeah. And she's the only girl," Tim answered. He was grinning, and he looked sort of proud. "But she's staying in the girls' dorm."

Waldo looked relieved. He carefully stacked up his roll sheets and picked up another set of papers. "These are the curfew rules," he began.

Jake groaned, and a few of us snickered. Waldo looked at us silently over the top of his glasses. When we were finally quiet he continued reading to us. "Everyone must be in his dormitory room

34

by ten o'clock in the evening. All meals will be taken in the dorm cafeteria—"

Jake made some barfing noises, and Waldo again waited patiently while we all cracked up.

"—unless you have obtained an off-campus pass from your dorm captain." He pushed the glasses up his nose for the fiftieth time and smiled. "That's me."

We just stared blankly at him and blinked our eyes like sick camels.

Waldo stood up. "You may all go to breakfast now," he said.

I followed Jake and Tim to the cafeteria.

"Could you believe that Waldo guy?" Jake said to Tim. "He should have been one of the extras for *Aliens.*"

Our practice that morning was a little more interesting than yesterday's. At least we were allowed to try some shots against an opponent. One player would dribble the ball for a lay-up while the defensive player guarded the basket, trying to block the shot or steal the ball away.

I was pretty nervous, because I really wanted to make a good impression on the coach. But, as luck would have it, the first person to guard me was Bobby. Cripes! As if I weren't shook up enough already.

I dribbled the ball a few times and then tried to

drive right, but Bobby blocked me off, forcing me to dribble with my left hand, which wasn't worth much—with or without a basketball in it. I stumbled and tried to cross the ball back over to my right hand, but she snatched the ball away.

"Good grab!" someone yelled at her. Bobby grinned at me and crinkled up her nose.

"Next!" yelled Coach White. "Crane—you guard Lambert this time."

I ducked my head down in a nod to the coach. Then I watched Jake dribble his magic ball onto the court. This is it, I thought. We'll see what old Buzz-Head can do with his magic ball today.

Jake dribbled twice and then made a head fake to the left. Like an idiot, I went for the fake, and Jake lofted the ball right over my head and sank a clean shot. I didn't even glance up at him, because I was starting to get really angry. First Bobby made me look like a fool. Now Jake had pretty much finished off the job.

"Next!" hollered the coach. "Lorimer. You go in and guard Lambert."

Tim and Bobby both stepped forward. Then Bobby giggled.

"Which one?" she asked him.

The coach was momentarily confused. "Uh— Tim. Tim Lorimer," he stammered. Bobby shrugged and backstepped into the crowd. Then Tim came forward and planted himself right in front of Jake, his feet wide apart and bouncing slightly.

First Jake tried dribbling to the right. Then he dribbled to the left. But Tim was all over him, and Jake was getting a little flustered. The only thing left for him to try was to go straight up without a fake. Seeing what he was about to do, Tim jumped up to block the shot, but he was just a split second too late. We all watched in silence as Jake's ball spun crazily and then dropped through the net without a sound.

Jake had just popped a perfect twelve-footer! I was convinced now. That wild shot should never have even made it to the rim. Jake's ball had to be magic.

By lunchtime, the entire cafeteria was buzzing with the news. Jake Lambert had a magic ball. He couldn't miss. He hadn't missed a single shot this morning!

But, if you ask me, it was Jake's arm that was magic. And all of us, I think, were hoping that a little of this "magic" would rub off on us.

So I have to admit that I now enjoyed sitting at the same table with Jake Lambert. Even the volleyball and soccer players eyed us with new respect as they trudged by with their bright orange lunch trays. I smiled kindly and waved at them, like royalty waving to the peasants.

Jake just grinned his lizard grin and tried to balance a spoon on the end of his nose. "I'm too good for this place," he laughed, poking me in the side with his elbow. I laughed too.

Then we both caught sight of Bobby getting in line with Charlotte Nass. Bobby and Charlotte were roommates, and they were getting pretty chummy. In fact, at breakfast this morning the two of them had walked right by without saying a word to me. But they both had big smiles for Jake, I noticed.

Jake put down his spoon and glanced over at me. "Get a load of Mutt and Jeff!" he howled, pointing to Bobby and Charlotte as they made their way through the food line. Bobby was short, and she bounced on her toes a lot. Next to her, Charlotte looked sort of like the Incredible Hulk.

"Oh, that's just Bobby Lorimer and Charlotte Nass," I said to Jake, pretending to be uninterested.

"Charlotte Nass? Don't you mean Charlotte MASS?" We both started chuckling, and Tim just shook his head at us.

"Lay off," Tim said quietly. "Charlotte's all right."

Jake looked at Tim, but he didn't say anything. Then he studied Charlotte and Bobby for a few moments.

39

"Well, your sister's pretty cute!" he finally remarked, stuffing half a hamburger into one cheek and chewing it like a wad of tobacco.

Suddenly I hated Jake Lambert, the way I would hate a rival. Then I told myself that was ridiculous. I mean, why would I want Bobby Lorimer hanging around me anyway? She was just a girl. And a pest! Jake was two years older than she was. He wouldn't want her hanging around either.

Or would he?

Bobby and Charlotte passed in front of our table, their trays loaded up.

"Hi!" Bobby greeted us, doing her famous nose crinkle. Was I just imagining things, or was she smiling directly at Jake?

"Good defense this morning, Bobby," Jake said.

Bobby giggled and shook her head. Charlotte, who had been staring down at her tray, raised her eyes.

"Bobby IS pretty good," she said.

When Jake didn't bother to answer her, Charlotte jutted her chin out and gave him that same defiant look she had aimed at me, right after flattening my foot in the parking lot.

Charlotte turned and smiled nervously at Tim. "Isn't she, Tim?"

Tim laughed and shrugged. "You're right about

that, Charlotte," he said, smiling at her. Then he grinned over at Bobby. "But it runs in the family."

"Well, she sure had Crane stumbling around the court today!" Jake continued, giving me a nudge with the end of his spoon.

A few of the other guys at our table started to snicker. I could feel my face heating up, but I grinned back at them, just to let everyone know that being pulverized on a basketball court in front of everyone at camp didn't bother me one bit.

"Let's go sit down, Bobby. I'm starved," Charlotte said loudly. Bobby nodded, and the two of them turned to leave.

"Hey, Crane! How come your face is all red?" jabbed Jake. That really made all the guys crack up even more, but I just kept on smiling like an idiot. It felt like my face was frozen.

As our whole table watched Charlotte and Bobby set down their trays, Jake slammed his fist squarely on the table, toppling my milk carton.

"Hey! I have a great idea to try out at breakfast!" he yelled. Then he whispered something into Joe Minelli's ear, and a slow smile spread across Joe's face.

I should have known then that any idea of Jake's would only get us into trouble.

6

Jake's great idea went something like this: A group of us would sit in a single row of chairs near the entrance to the cafeteria. Each guy would have a set of scorecards on his lap, kind of like the judges in a gymnastics or ice-skating competition. Only we would be judging the people coming through the door. When all the other kids started filing in for breakfast, we would hold up our scorecards for everyone else to see. Simple. Fun.

Two days later Jake was ready to try his idea out. He woke me up at six-thirty and slapped a felt marker and eleven sheets of blank paper on top of my chest.

I was too sleepy to really think about what I was about to do, but I followed Jake to the cafeteria anyway. There was something about Jake that

42

was contagious—sort of like measles or chicken pox. He was just so sure that this was going to be a lot of fun, that he had managed to get seven of us to go along with him. Of course, at six-thirty in the morning his idea didn't seem as enjoyable, and a couple of the guys started grumbling.

"Oh, come on. This is going to be a blast!" Jake hooted, showing us his scorecards. "Just hold up a number whenever someone walks into the cafeteria. Ten is a perfect score."

"Why do we have eleven cards then?" Terry Merrill asked sleepily. He was still wearing his pajama top, and it was on inside out.

"For zero," Jake said slowly, waving his zero card right under Terry's nose. He laughed loudly, and we all joined in.

Someone tapped me on the shoulder with a Magic Marker, and I turned around.

"Hey, this is kind of fun," Steve Crawford said shyly to me. His red hair was sticking straight up on one side of his head. Jake had recruited Steve at the last minute because the eighth "judge" had decided to skip breakfast this morning and sleep in.

"Yeah . . . but what if no one comes to breakfast?" I asked, grinning at him.

Steve just shrugged and laughed. "Who cares?"

"Does anybody really win this contest?" asked Joe Minelli. "Because I have a great idea for a trophy."

43

"Like what?" Jake shouted back at him. "Your dirty socks?"

Everyone started laughing, and Joe pretended to look hurt. "I only wore them once," he pouted. Then he cracked up too.

We lined up our chairs by the door at seven-fifteen. I stifled a yawn. I was too tired to feel hungry yet.

The first two people to walk through the door were a girl from the soccer team and a lanky black guy from our own basketball camp named Jim. The girl started giggling when we held up our scorecards for Jim: 8-7-9-8-9-9-7-2. The two was Jake's.

"TWO!" Jim shouted at Jake. "Who are you calling a two?" But he was laughing as he passed in front of our row of chairs.

Jake grinned at him. "It's that ugly jacket, man," he yelled back. "I had to take off eight points from a perfect ten for that!" Then he turned to me. "Hey, this is some fun, huh? They love it!"

A couple of guys from our hall walked in just then, rubbing their eyes sleepily.

"Those two still have mattress hair!" Jake shouted. As if on cue, we all held up our score-cards again: 2-3-3-2-7-2-3-2. Steve, who was hold-ing the seven, grinned timidly at us. "I like

44

mattress hair," he said quietly. We all laughed, and Jake punched Steve in the arm.

The next person to enter was probably the prettiest girl at the whole camp. Her name was Michelle Reiker. She was a gymnast with long blonde hair that swished back and forth perfectly when she walked. Up went the cards: 9-10-10-10-4-9-9-10.

Steve shrugged at us again and put the four facedown in his lap. "I still like mattress hair," he said with a crooked smile. Joe Minelli whacked Steve on the head with one of his scorecards, and we all howled.

Then two girls from the volleyball team shuffled in. One of them yawned at us.

"Man! Who let those two loose?" Jake hollered. The yawner opened her eyes wide enough to glare back at him.

"Just ignore them," her friend warned, but by this time it was as if our scorecards had minds of their own: 2-3-3-1-3-2-1-2.

"What's all that supposed to mean?" asked the yawner. She was pointing and glaring at us now.

"It's their IQ scores," snapped the other girl. "Doubled!"

"Very funny!" Jake called out after them. "Why don't you two go back to your cage before the zookeeper finds out you're missing!" All eight of us laughed as if we had never had so much fun in our lives.

Actually, I really was having fun—until Bobby passed through the double doors. For some reason it felt weird to be giving Bobby a number. I mean, she was my friend, even if she did run all over me on the basketball courts. And I suddenly felt funny judging her.

But, before I had time to think, we flashed our cards at her: 9-7-8-9-9-8-10-9.

Bobby froze and gaped at the eight of us with her mouth hanging open. Then she shoved her hands down on her hips and thrust her head forward. She reminded me of a rooster getting ready for a cockfight.

"What gives you the right to judge everybody else, you male chauvinist piglets!" she shouted across the entire length of the cafeteria.

Jake laughed hysterically and started making snorting noises like a pig. A few of us joined in. Since Jake was laughing at Bobby, I felt that I had to laugh even harder, just to show him that I was as cool as he was.

Then Charlotte plodded into the cafeteria right behind Bobby, unaware of the commotion Bobby had started. A few of the guys started snickering, and suddenly all I could think about was the way Charlotte always called me "kid."

Up went the cards again: 3-3-2-1-3-2-0. Of course, that wasn't all of the cards, but I didn't realize it then.

I wish now that I could go back in time and leave my stupid scorecard in my lap too—just like Jake did. Because I hate to admit this, but I was the "zero flasher."

I don't know why I did it. No. That's not true. I do know. I did it because I was mad at Charlotte for calling me "kid" and knocking my breath away with those backslaps of hers. And I did it because I thought Bobby wanted to be my friend, but she was always hanging around with King Kong Charlotte instead. Let's face it: I was sick of seeing Bobby and Charlotte teamed up together all the time like Batman and Robin.

I looked at Charlotte over the top of my scorecard. She was just studying each number painfully and silently, until she got to my zero. Her brown eyes were wide open at first, and they stopped evenly with mine for a moment. Then her face just sort of squeezed itself together real tight.

Charlotte didn't bother to pick up a breakfast tray. She just let out one sob before she turned and fled out the doors and down the steps.

All the judges were feeling a little uneasy, since the traffic was now backed up at the door. I don't think anyone else wanted to walk into the cafe-

teria right now. At least, not with us sitting there like door guards. Slowly, we all turned the scores facedown in our laps.

I glanced sideways at Jake. If he had been looking at me, I think I would have slugged him in the face. But he and Joe were giggling and slapping stupidly at each other.

Bobby started to run after Charlotte, then stopped and turned around. "You guys are all idiots!" she shouted, stamping one of her dirty sneakers on the floor.

She charged right up to me, her pointy little nose almost touching mine. "You must like to think you're funny, Leslie Crane," she said to me. "Well, you don't hear ME laughing!"

Then Bobby was gone. I watched the double doors of the cafeteria swinging behind her. I was the judge who had given her a ten, but I didn't really think she had noticed. In fact, it probably would have just made her angrier at me.

I stared straight ahead and blinked a few times. Then I started to stack up my scorecards and fold up the chair. Our little game was definitely over.

Joe and Jake began whispering together. I didn't even try to listen.

Terry Merrill picked up his cards and shrugged at me. "I'm going back to bed," he muttered.

Steve just left his cards on the chair. "Me too," he said.

I nodded at them but didn't follow right away. I didn't feel like talking to anyone anyway. After walking halfway across the lawn, I felt a tap on my shoulder. It was Tim Lorimer.

"You know, you guys are really dumb jerks," he said. I heard myself suck in a breath. If Tim had punched me in the stomach I don't think it could have hurt as much. Fighting back the wetness that was welling up behind my eyeballs, I watched Tim charge off in the direction of the basketball courts.

Then Jake ran up behind me and slapped me on the back.

"Don't mind Tim," he said reassuringly. "He's just an old lady. He'll get over it."

"Darn you, Jake!" I shouted, stopping in my tracks. "First you get Bobby mad at me, and now Charlotte. Man! One hard swat from her could put me in the hospital."

"Hey, Crane," Jake said with a laugh. "Don't blame me. I wasn't the one holding up your scorecard, you know."

He was right. I had dug myself into this hole. And I didn't know how to climb back out. What I wanted right now was a good long talk with my mom, along with some of her banana bread and a big glass of cold milk.

I wished I were anywhere but here. What was the use, anyway? After all, I didn't have to play basketball for the rest of my life, and I knew it. If I got desperate enough, I could always buy one of those long metal detectors and search for nickels and dimes buried in the sand at the beach.

In my mind I could still hear Bobby yelling at me, and Charlotte sobbing as she ran out the door. It was the first time I had ever seen Charlotte with her chin down, and I began to realize that when it came back up, I would deserve whatever I had coming to me. I felt even meaner than the Grinch who stole Christmas.

No one seemed to be around, which suited me just fine. So, I headed straight to my room. I don't know how long I was there, but eventually I realized that our morning practice was about to start. Oh, crumbs! Now I was going to have to polish the floor for Coach White, on top of everything else.

Waldo peeked his head around the door. "You have a phone call," he said, looking at his watch, "but practice starts in five minutes. It's your little brother."

I jumped out of bed and shoved myself through the doorway and around Waldo without even thanking him.

"Hello?"

"Hi, Les. It's Cam."

"Hi, Cam. What is it now?"

"Well, I was just wondering. . . . Is there another way I could get some money? Fast?"

I almost hung up on him, but then something hit me. "I've got an idea," I said quickly.

"What?"

"Why don't you get yourself a metal detector?"

"Huh?"

"You know. Those long things that the men use at the beach."

"You mean the men looking for money? In the sand?"

"Yeah."

Cam didn't say anything for a while. "Can you give me enough money to buy one?"

I stood there in the hall, looking at the receiver. Maybe I should have hung up on him.

"Look, I gotta go, Cam. I'm late for practice."

"Well, if you think of anything else, will you call me?" He paused. "It's kind of lonely in our room with just Max."

I glanced at the clock in the hall. One minute until practice. "Yes," I said quickly. "I'll call you."

"Okay. Bye."

"Good-bye, Cam."

I ran all the way to the gym and reached the courts just as Coach White was blowing his whistle.

7

By lunchtime my stomach was rumbling with animal-like noises. I hadn't eaten a thing at breakfast. And our morning workout had drained me of all my strength, especially since I was dribbling wide to avoid running into Bobby on the court.

It didn't matter. Bobby wouldn't even look my way during our lay-up drills. To make matters worse, Jake's magic ball swished through the hoop clean as a whistle every time he took a shot.

I spied Jake talking to Bobby over by the drinking fountain when the drills were finished, and she looked pretty angry. I wondered what Jake was saying to her. He was probably trying to convince Bobby that he had been the only judge with any feelings this morning. After all, he had spared Charlotte by not giving her a score, hadn't he?

Ha! I knew darn well that the real reason Jake

didn't hold up a scorecard for Charlotte was because he hadn't even seen her come in the door! Jake had been too busy trying to impress Bobby and snorting like a pig to notice.

I trudged back to the dorm wondering about lunch. Now don't get me wrong. I was so hungry by this time that I actually felt kind of dizzy. But there was no way I was going to show my face in that cafeteria! Not this soon, anyway.

I walked past the phone in the hall and glanced at the pile of mail lying on the table. Right on top was a letter from my mom.

Mom! She still loved me, even if everyone else thought I was a creep. I ripped the letter open and ran all the way to my room to read it.

Dear Les,

How are things at camp? I'm sure you're having a great time. Everything is just about the same around here. Susie will be going back home to Michigan next week. She's very upset about it. The poor little thing! She even gave Cam a picture to remember her by until she returns next summer. Isn't that adorable? A little romance has blossomed right here on Sand Hill Drive!

Enclosed is a twenty-dollar bill, just in case you need some spending money. I love you.

Mom

An adorable little romance, I thought disgustedly. I didn't want to hear anything about a little romance, adorable or not. What I really wanted to know about was the important stuff! Like, was Cam making Play-Doh dinosaurs without me now? And how was Dad coping with the lawn, now that I wasn't there to mow it the right way? Was Mom making Cam's favorite kind of cookies now? Did Mike find someone else to play one-on-one?

Didn't anyone even *miss* me? She hadn't said one thing about that!

I crumpled up the letter and threw it into the wastebasket—after taking out the twenty-dollar bill. But I was wishing that Mom could be here right now, wrapping her arms around me, with her giggly little laugh, and letting me know that I wasn't really the rottenest kid in the world.

I stared at the twenty-dollar bill in my hand. Here, at least, was the answer to my lunch problem. I could buy something to eat. But first, I had to request a pass from Waldo, which meant I had to go to his room.

When I walked through the door, Waldo looked up at me over the top of his glasses. He was reading one of his books, filled with tiny printed words and drawings that looked like Egyptian hieroglyphics.

"Yes?" he mumbled, clearly distracted at my interruption.

"I want to go to McDonald's for lunch," I answered.

Waldo blinked at me from behind his thick lenses.

"So I need a pass," I said slowly.

Waldo riffled through one of his drawers and drew out a pink slip of paper. Before signing it, he asked, "How long are you planning to be gone?"

When I didn't answer right away, he handed me the pass and then tapped his pen lightly on the desk.

"About an hour," I muttered, shrugging my shoulders. Then I turned and headed quickly for the door.

"Hey, Leslie—" he said, as I was almost out of the room. "I heard about Jake's little stunt at breakfast."

I froze, ready for his big speech on judging other people. I didn't think I could stand that right now.

"I decided not to tell your coach," Waldo said. He was looking at me intently, and it gave me the jitters. What did he expect me to say anyway?

"Do you have anything to say?" he asked quietly.

I just shook my head and shoved the pink pass into my pocket. How could I tell Waldo about the look on Charlotte's face and the way that Bobby had yelled at me in front of everyone in the cafeteria?

Waldo stared at me for a few seconds more. Then he looked back down at his book without another word. I made a quick exit.

I figured that Coach White had probably heard about our "contest" anyway. But Waldo could have refused to give me the lunch pass, especially since I hadn't even bothered to give him a good reason. Maybe Waldo wasn't so bad after all, I told myself. I mean, at least he wasn't a snitch.

While I nibbled on my quarter pounder with cheese, I watched a young girl stuffing a ketchup-smeared french fry into her mommy's mouth. Through the window I observed a boy about my own age helping his little brother down a slide. It reminded me of all the evenings my dad and I had tried to teach Cam how to ride a bike. Maybe Dad was even planning to give my brother a lesson tonight—without me there to help!

In that hot smelly McDonald's, I discovered the true meaning of loneliness.

Feeling miserable, I bit into my hot apple turnover and immediately let out a muffled yell. They weren't kidding about these turnovers being hot! Now the roof of my mouth was burned so badly I couldn't even taste anything. In disgust, I threw the turnover back down onto my tray. I contemplated suicide.

That reminded me of a story my mom loved to tell her friends. Just to humiliate me. It seems that my mother had been very concerned about my mental state after Cam was born. I think her worries began after I pushed Cam out of his baby swing.

So Mom visited a child psychiatrist for some advice. He told her to have me draw some pictures at home and she could bring them back for him to study. He then proceeded to show her some examples of pictures that had been drawn by extremely disturbed children.

One picture really bothered my mother a lot. It was a crayon drawing of a little boy's body. The head was there too. But it just wasn't connected to the rest of him.

"What does that one mean?" Mom asked the psychiatrist in horror.

"Oh, that child is suicidal," the psychiatrist answered.

Well, I did draw some pictures for my mother and . . . you guessed it! In one of them, my head was floating in the air about six inches away from my neck.

"OH MY GOD!" Mom shrieked, grabbing my head between her two hands and shoving my face into her chest. "What is this?"

"Oh, it's just me. Laughing my head off," I answered, grinning up at her.

Mom threw the doctor's phone number away.

Thinking of that story now sort of made me smile. I realized that there were two ways to look at anything. Sure, I could really be suicidal. Or I could just be a happy guy laughing my head off. It all depended on how you looked at the picture.

And I figured I could take this Charlotte situation the same way. I could either face up to her and apologize, or I could just try to avoid her for a week and a half.

Of course, Charlotte had a choice too. She could either accept my apology or refuse it. I thought about those breath-stopping thumps on the back she could deliver and came to a quick decision. I chose solution number two: avoidance.

It was almost one o'clock now. I jogged all the way back to the gym so I wouldn't be late for our afternoon practice. The air was so hot my teeth felt dry.

And when I got to the courts I was feeling pretty sick. I mean, who wouldn't after jogging five blocks in the heat with a quarter pounder and half of a hot apple turnover in his stomach? I decided that maybe the cafeteria wasn't so bad in comparison.

After our afternoon drills Jake and Tim headed straight for the cafeteria to eat an early dinner.

"Hey, Crane. Are you coming?" Jake asked.

"Not now," I said with a shrug. "I'll be there later."

Tim looked like he was about to say something, but then Jake nudged him, and they both took off in the direction of the cafeteria.

I watched them walk past the dorm building. Jake was laughing and making hand gestures. Tim wasn't saying much. To tell the truth, it looked like he was listening mostly, with his hands down at his sides.

I knew I had to keep a low profile, and I had already decided that a disguise at dinner might help, just in case I bumped into Charlotte Nass. This was my chance.

I ran to the dorm and searched through all my clothes for anything that would mask my identity at dinner tonight. Considering that I had packed for only two weeks, there wasn't much to choose from.

I spent a little time digging around in my dresser drawers, but by six-thirty I was finally ready. Even though it was still about eighty degrees outside, I wore my light blue sweat suit into the cafeteria, with the hood pulled up and tied real tight, so that not much of my face showed. On top of that, I wore a white baseball cap.

To complete my disguise I added a pair of sunglasses, so that I wouldn't have to look at anyone directly. I know that I looked like Papa Smurf going to a beach party, but at least no one recognized me in the food line.

Some kids gave me funny looks, though, and I heard one guy joking about my sunglasses. As I looked for a seat, I noticed that two of this morning's judges were sitting alone. I figured none of us was very popular company right now.

I found an empty table and slid quietly into the metal chair. Then I started to twirl some spaghetti onto my fork. I saw Michelle Reiker pass by my table, her blonde hair swishing from side to side. Some guy was walking behind her, lugging two dinner trays.

"Check that guy out," Michelle giggled. "It's Mr. Hollywood!"

"Looks more like a reject from the Winter Olympics," snickered the guy with the trays. "What's the matter, buddy? Did you take a wrong turn on your way to the bobsleds?"

I continued twirling my spaghetti until they were gone. I didn't really even taste the food, but I kept on chewing it anyway. It was something to do.

Even though my ears were covered up, I could make out certain familiar sounds in the cafeteria. Sounds like chairs being pulled out from the tables, dinner trays being dumped into the bins, and kids laughing and talking to each other.

Then I heard a sound that was unmistakable. Bobby's giggle. And it was coming from directly behind me.

"I couldn't believe Jake this afternoon," Bobby was saying. "No one could stop him."

"Not even Tim?" asked another voice.

Oh, no! Charlotte! Bobby and Charlotte were pulling out two seats at the table right behind mine! I really didn't want to be there, but if I got up and ran, I'd be recognized for sure. I froze.

I couldn't make out what Bobby said next. It was something about Tim and Charlotte. But I could hear Charlotte loud and clear as usual. She laughed at something Bobby said, and then there was a pause. I figured they were probably both chewing or something.

"Oh, come on, Charlotte!" Bobby finally whispered a little louder. "Haven't you ever been kissed by a boy?"

I should have gotten up right then and walked out, but I kept listening. In fact, I moved my chair back a couple of inches so I wouldn't miss a word.

"Never!" Charlotte breathed. "Have you?"

"Just once."

What! I almost turned my head around, but the hood of my sweatshirt was too tight, and the zipper scraped my neck.

"Who was it?" I heard Charlotte whisper.

"Some guy in my fourth-grade class."

"What did you do?"

"I felt like throwing up," Bobby answered. "It was absolutely gross!"

"I know what you mean," Charlotte agreed. "The lips and all. . . ."

"But now I practice sometimes at home," Bobby added.

Oh, Jeez! I shouldn't be listening to this. I really had to get out of here! But how?

"With Scotch tape," Bobby continued. "It's sticky, so if you close your eyes, it kind of feels like someone is kissing you back."

I groaned loudly, and I guess Bobby heard me, because she whipped her head around and spoke to me.

"What's your problem, buddy?" she asked angrily. "Haven't you heard that eavesdropping is very rude?"

"I wasn't eavesdropping!" I replied, turning around to face her. "Is it my fault you're talking loud enough to be picked up by radar scanners in Russia?" I could make out Charlotte's face behind Bobby's head. She looked sort of embarrassed, but curious about what her roommate was going to do next.

Bobby was just plain angry. At first her eyes were sort of squinting at me. But then they grew

63

wide with instant recognition. She knew who I was, even under the Smurf hood and the baseball hat. And Bobby began to giggle.

"Bobby!" Charlotte called out behind her. "Who is that?"

"Oh, it's just Leslie Crane." Bobby laughed.

Charlotte looked at me uncomfortably. I shrugged and slowly took off the cap and the glasses. Then I untied the string on my sweatshirt and let the hood fall down around my shoulders.

"It's just me," I responded, flashing her a lopsided smile. I realized that avoiding Charlotte was not going to be as easy as I had thought. So I decided to go ahead with solution number one. The big apology.

I figured this was the perfect time to let Charlotte know how really sorry I felt about what had happened this morning, so I just licked my lips and opened my mouth. I wanted to get this over with as quickly as possible.

"Look, Charlotte, I'm—"

"We're not talking to you, Leslie," Bobby said, crinkling up her nose.

Charlotte looked at Bobby and then at me. She was frowning slightly. "That's right," she said finally.

Charlotte stood up and walked around the table. Then she made a face at me. "That's some costume, kid," she said.

Charlotte and Bobby turned in unison and trotted toward the girl's bathroom, leaving their half-empty trays behind. I picked up my cap and sunglasses, watching them go. Then I dumped my tray.

Yeah, it's just me, I thought gloomily, as I thrust both hands deep into my pockets. It's just me, Leslie Crane. Laughing my head off.

8

I arrived at our practice late the next morning. Jake and Tim had gotten up early and gone to breakfast, but I wasn't hungry. Besides, terrible things always seemed to happen to me whenever I set foot in that cafeteria.

Coach White looked at me as I walked into the gym, but he didn't say a word. He just gave two sharp whistle blasts and pointed to the far court where Bobby, Jake, and Steve were practicing lay-ups.

"Well, if it isn't our new floor polisher," Joe Minelli said as I passed him. I walked straight ahead.

"Hey, little buddy," said Jake, giving me the high five. "It's lay-ups and passing drills this morning." Then he rolled his eyes and said

"BOOOOORING" very loudly, to let all of us know just how he felt about doing drills.

"Hi, Les," Steve said, passing the ball to me. "You go ahead. I'll guard."

"Okay." I let the ball bounce a couple of times, just to get the feel of it. Then I looked up at the hoop and drove to Steve's right. He zipped by me and snatched the ball away in mid-bounce, whipping it in closer to the basket for a clear shot. The ball gently banked off the backboard, just above the rim, and dropped through the net without a sound.

Coach White stood right behind me. "You took your eye off the ball, Crane. Try it again. Bobby Lorimer, you take defense."

Oh, no! Bobby was going to guard me now. That's just what I needed!

I dribbled the ball, keeping my eye on it this time. Then I faked to the left, and Bobby went for the fake. I drove by her before she had time to recover and went straight up toward the basket. I'm going to make this shot, I thought excitedly to myself. But then Bobby jumped up in front of me and slammed the ball away from the net.

Jake hooted loudly. "Way to go, Bobby! Great defense!" he yelled.

But that wasn't the worst of it. I came down right on top of Bobby's left foot.

"Ouch! Watch where you put those planks,

68

Pencil Neck!" Bobby shook her head angrily, but I noticed she was talking to me again—sort of. I opened my mouth to apologize to her.

"SHREEEEK!" A whistle shrilled, cutting me off.

"All of you into center court," shouted Coach White. "Zone defense first. Then the full-court press."

Coach White quickly divided us up into two teams. Luckily, Bobby was on my side, so I didn't have to trample all over her feet trying to guard her.

Jake had the ball, and he was heading directly for the area Bobby was supposed to cover. I watched him dribble three times before I noticed that the ball he was handling wasn't the "magic" one.

"Where is Jake's ball?" I whispered to Steve.

"Coach took it. He said we all had to play with the same ball."

I nodded, running after Jake just as he drove through to the basket, going for a jump shot. The ball left his hand a little too soon, bouncing off the rim and out of bounds.

"Hey, I thought you never missed, Lambert!" Joe hollered at him.

"Lay off!" Jake shouted back. The rest of us just laughed. I think we were all relieved to see Jake miss. He didn't do it very often.

I glanced over at Bobby, but she wasn't laugh-

69

ing at all. Her eyes were studying Jake carefully, and her nose was all crinkled up in concentration. I hoped she was only watching his style, trying to figure out how he could really be so good. And maybe wondering why he had missed this time. I mean, it sort of bugged me that Bobby was paying any attention to Jake at all. And I just had to grit my teeth as I watched Jake grin broadly at her and dance his little shuffle.

When the coach's whistle finally shrilled at noon, I was ready to quit. My stomach felt hollow, and my legs were throbbing.

I filled up my tray in the cafeteria and went to find a seat. As I sat down, I noticed Jake over at a table near the window. He was talking to Bobby and Tim, but I couldn't see what Bobby was doing, because her back was facing me. When Jake finally left their table, Tim and Bobby got up to empty their trays.

Charlotte walked right by me without a word, but I don't think she even saw me because she was heading straight for Bobby and Tim. She said something to the two of them, and then they all laughed loudly.

I watched them miserably, taking little nibbles of my hamburger and chewing slowly. The burger was horrible. It tasted like rubber and pickles in a bun, but I kept on eating. And watching.

"Mind if I join you?" someone asked behind

70

me. Waldo pulled out a chair and sat down next to me. He glanced over at my tray. "No Mc-Donald's today?"

"No," I answered gloomily, without looking at him. I was still staring over at the other table.

Waldo picked up a fork and began digging around in his tuna salad. Every once in a while he would pull the fork out and dump a couple of pieces of celery on a paper napkin.

He stopped picking and looked up at me. I guess he could feel me watching him. "The strings get stuck in my throat," he explained.

Waldo was looking at me thoughtfully, and I was afraid he was going to pat me on the head or something.

"Is something bothering you, Crane?" he asked, studying me from behind those heavy glasses. And for one crazy moment I actually considered telling him everything: about Jake getting me into that stupid contest and Bobby yelling at me, and about Tim calling me a jerk and Charlotte not speaking to me anymore. Then I just picked up my rubber-burger and took a big bite.

"No," I lied.

"Well," he said, picking up his tray, "let me know if there is. That's why I'm here." Waldo sounded concerned, and it made me feel bad that I didn't want to talk to him. But I just couldn't.

I guess I must have looked pretty awful too.

71

Maybe Waldo was afraid I might be getting sick or something. When you're a dorm captain, you have to worry about stuff like that. He finally stood up, but he leaned his head down, so that his face was almost level with mine.

"The door to my room is always open," he said.

"Yeah." I ate the rest of my hamburger and watched him walk out the door.

The afternoon practice went a little better for me. Steve and I were working together on jump shots, and I sank most of mine, even with him pressing in pretty close.

Coach White blew his whistle, and we all stopped to look at him. "Let's switch partners," he yelled out. "Defensive players, rotate to the right."

Bobby walked over to my court and planted herself right under the basket. There was a long silence. The moment kind of stretched out between us like a rubber band. Bobby didn't utter a word to me, and I didn't really know what to say to her.

So I just didn't say anything. I'm not kidding! Bobby and I played against each other for twenty minutes and never made a sound. It was sort of eerie, if you ask me. Like playing basketball with a ghost.

When the coach finally blew his whistle again, I

grabbed the ball and held it up to my chest. I looked straight at Bobby and took a deep breath. She was looking back at me, blinking rapidly.

"Bobby . . ." It was a plea.

"Rotate right!" shouted Coach White.

Bobby crinkled her nose at me and sort of pranced over to Jake's court on her tiptoes. I watched her go, wondering if she might have been about to answer me. What was going on in her head anyway, I thought. With girls, you could never tell.

The basketball that I had been clutching slowly fell from my grasp and hit the floor, rolling over Joe Minelli's foot.

"Wake up, Les," he laughed. "You've got some REAL competition now."

Angrily, I grabbed the ball and put up a shot, right over Joe's head.

And I missed.

"Hey, Crane!" Jake hollered through the bathroom door that evening. "You've got another phone call. It's that kid again!"

Cam? What did he want now? Another raise? I finished brushing my teeth and rushed out to the telephone in the hall.

"This is Les," I said into the receiver.

"Hi. It's me."

"What do you want?"

73

"Well, I was wondering if maybe I could borrow your bike." This kid was unbelievable! I had been gone only a few days and he already had my hamster and an IOU for thirteen dollars. Now he wanted my bicycle too.

"My bike!" I said to him. "But you already have a bike."

"Ummmmm . . ."

"Don't you?"

"Well, I loaned it to Susie."

"Why in the world did you do that?"

"Because she just wants to play dolls all the time. I thought if she had a bike, then maybe we could do something else—like go bike riding."

"But do you even know how to ride a bike?" I paused. "Does Susie?"

"Dad's been helping us."

I felt my own sudden tears welling up. Dad was giving lessons to Cam without me. He was even giving lessons to Susie Walker, and she would be gone in a week! I wasn't necessary anymore. It looked like no one cared that I was gone.

"Now, let me get this straight," I said slowly. "You want to have my bike so that Susie can have *yours?*"

"Yeah."

Two guys stopped in front of me, signaling that they wanted to use the phone.

"Look," I said hurriedly to Cam, "why don't

74

you just knock out a couple more of your teeth? The way you keep upping the price on them, you could probably buy yourself a brand new bike in no time."

There was silence on the other end. For a minute I thought Cam had hung up on me. Then I heard him breathing.

I sighed heavily. "Okay, Cam. You can ride my bike, but only until Susie goes home. And only if Dad is with you."

Cam still didn't say a word.

"Do you understand me, Cam?"

"Yes," he answered quietly.

I thought our conversation was over because my brother didn't say anything else. "Well, bye," I said, starting to hang up.

"No, Les. Wait!"

Now what did he want? My skateboard and catcher's mitt too? "What is it, Cam?" I snapped. Then I shrugged helplessly at the two guys still waiting for the phone.

"I wish you were back home, Les," Cam said.

I swallowed a couple of times and put the receiver up close to my mouth. "I wish I was too, Cam," I whispered.

9

I got up early the next morning. No way was I going to miss breakfast three days in a row! Especially if Bobby was going to be guarding me in practice again today.

Jake's bed was empty, and his shoes were gone. That meant he was probably already in the cafeteria.

As I was tying my high tops, Tim slowly raised himself up onto one elbow and looked over at me sleepily.

"You going to breakfast?" he asked.

"Yeah," I muttered, afraid that Tim still thought I was a jerk.

"Can you wait a minute? I'll come too."

"Sure."

Tim threw on a pair of gray sweatpants and a

white T-shirt. His hair looked perfect, even after he had just jumped out of bed.

"Tim?" I asked, gathering up some courage. "Are you still mad at me?"

Tim laughed. "Maybe a little."

"Is your sister ever going to talk to me again?"

Tim shrugged. "She talks to Jake, doesn't she?"

"Yeah. But why?" As far as I was concerned, Jake deserved the silent treatment a lot more than I did.

"At least he tried to explain to her—"

"And Bobby believed him?"

"I didn't say that. I just said he *tried*. That's worth something, isn't it?"

When I didn't answer, Tim plopped down on the edge of his bed, looking straight at me. "Les, why don't you just apologize to Charlotte?"

"That's easy for you to say!" I responded gloomily. "Bobby won't even let me near enough to talk to Charlotte. I think her man-to-man defense drills are really paying off!"

Tim laughed. "You guys better make up before school starts."

"Why?"

"Because you're both going to be together next year in middle school."

I gulped. And Bobby would be there too. "Oh, yeah," was all I said.

"Just explain to Charlotte about Jake," Tim suggested. "It may seem like he's magic sometimes, but everyone knows he's just a potato head."

Tim was right. All I had to do was apologize. Why hadn't I tried that again? Because I didn't really want to find out what Charlotte Nass thought about me. Let's be honest: I was scared to death of what she might say.

The door flew open, and Mr. Potato Head himself burst into the room.

"Crane!" he exclaimed, pointing a finger at me. "I need your help."

Tim slipped around Jake, into the doorway. Then he crossed his eyes at me and pointed to the bathroom down the hall. I nodded, figuring I could catch up with him later.

"What kind of help?" I asked Jake doubtfully.

"You know there's a free movie in the cafeteria next week? For all the camp kids?"

"Sooooo?"

"So I asked Bobby to go with me."

Two whole minutes. That's how long it seemed before my mouth could move.

"And Bobby said she'd go with you?" I squeaked out finally.

"Yeah, sure." He grinned at me. "She said it's a free country, and I can sit wherever I want."

"And you want to sit with Bobby," I said simply.

"Right. But she's dragging old Charlotte MASS along with her."

I was afraid to find out what was next on Jake's mind.

"And . . ." he continued, " I want you to come too—and sit with Charlotte."

"What?" I shrieked. "Are you out of your mind? Charlotte doesn't want to see me anywhere! Except maybe at my own funeral."

I grabbed my sweatshirt and started for the door.

"If you come with me, I'll let you use my basketball," Jake offered, grinning slowly at me. "You know that it's magic."

I considered my choices. And, to be honest, I thought that ball would be kind of nice to have. Besides, I figured I had to go to the movie with them, just to keep an eye on Jake and Bobby.

But . . . I was terrified! What would I say to Charlotte? Worse than that, what would she say to me? Even Bobby's silent treatment was better than having to face that.

And Jake's last idea had gotten me into nothing but trouble! Then again, if I didn't go with them, who knew what Jake would say about me to Bobby? She could end up even angrier at me. I had to go along just to protect myself!

"Okay," I agreed reluctantly. "But this isn't a

date or anything, is it? I'm only eleven years old
. . . well . . . almost twelve."

"No way!" Jake assured me. "I just want you to
sit next to Charlotte so that I can sit with
Bobby." For some reason, I didn't like the sound
of this.

"What movie is it, anyway?" I grumbled.

"The Return of Zorg."

"But that's my movie!" I blurted out painfully.

"What do you mean your movie?" Jake
demanded.

"I—uh—I mean, it's my favorite movie," I stammered. How could I tell him that Bobby and Tim
had invited me to that same movie just a week
ago?

"You coming to breakfast or not?" Jake asked me.

"Not right now. I'm going with Tim."

"Well, I'll see you guys at practice then."

"Okay."

"Don't change your mind on me, Crane," he
added sharply.

I just nodded, sitting back down on my bed.
Then I leaned back against the pillow and looked
up at the ceiling. There was a crack running
across the middle of the plaster. The crack was all
crooked, and it looked like something that a kid
would scribble on paper.

Staring at that jagged line made me think about

the crayon drawing of me laughing my head off. And thinking about the drawing reminded me that some things can look terrifying at first and really turn out to be nothing at all.

Sitting next to Charlotte would be terrifying all right, but it would give me the chance to apologize to her. And even if she did tell me I was a rotten, no-good, lousy, mean creep, I could feel a little better about myself. Because I would know that I was a rotten, no-good, lousy, mean creep who had at least apologized.

Confused. That's what I really was. This camp was all mixed up. The kids that I wanted to be friends with didn't want to be friends with me, and the one kid who thought he was my friend really wasn't.

I lay there with my eyes closed. I was remembering what Cam had said to me last night on the phone, and I wished again that I could be back home. At least when I was there I knew who my friends were.

Maybe I would call my parents tonight, I thought. Talking to them might make me feel a little better. And I could even ask Mom for some advice. On that happy note, I got up and went to join Tim. After all, it was time for breakfast, and I was starving.

10

"Here!" Jake shouted from the corner of the court. I glanced at him, then passed the ball quickly to Tim, who was running up behind him. I set a screen for Tim and he took a shot, but the ball hit the far side of the rim and bounced off.

Jake rushed in for the rebound and leaped, tipping the ball over and in. He was really on this afternoon, I thought disgustedly. Jake had missed only one shot. And that was a wild throw from the perimeter that he made in desperation because Tim had been covering him too closely.

Tim's defense was usually pretty good, I thought to myself. But his shots still needed some work. Whenever Tim played offense, his aim was just a little short.

I got hold of the ball next, only to work myself into a corner, with Bobby jumping all over me.

So when I saw Tim make a drive for the center I threw him a hook pass. Without hesitating, he threw the ball up in a lopsided arc. It bounced off the rim, and Jake grabbed the rebound again.

"TWEEEET!" Coach White ran into the center of the court and took the ball away from Jake. Then he turned to Tim. "Lorimer, you've got to beat your man to the basket and stop throwing off-balance shots. That cost you two points."

Tim nodded, but he was staring down at the hardwood floor.

"Yeah. Your own sister can do better than that!" Jake snickered from behind the coach.

"That's enough, Lambert," Coach White warned, chewing on his whistle. "Let's take a break. Be back on the courts in fifteen minutes."

I sat down on the lower risers and Tim plopped down beside me, wiping a sweaty arm across his forehead.

Bobby charged over to us and sat down in a huff next to Tim. "That was really dumb—what Jake said to you!" Bobby said angrily.

Tim actually started to smile, which made Bobby even angrier. "He's just a big bully," she added.

When Tim didn't reply, Bobby turned suddenly to me. "Isn't he?"

I was so surprised to have Bobby ask my opinion about anything that I couldn't answer her either. She turned her head to look at Tim again.

"Well, you two sure are the brainy bunch today!" she exclaimed, getting up. "You make Jake look almost intelligent."

Tim and I watched Bobby stomp over to Jake and say something to him, her hands shoved angrily on her hips. Jake was grinning up at her, his head cocked to one side, and I found myself hating him again.

Tim began to chuckle. "With a sister like that, who needs enemies?" he laughed.

I smiled, trying to imagine my own little brother sticking up for me like that. And thinking about him made me wonder what he was doing right now. Cam and Susie Walker were probably sitting on our front lawn at this very moment, staring helplessly at the bikes they couldn't even ride. . . .

Helpless? I should have known that my little brother was never helpless. That night Cam called me for the fourth time.

"I asked Mom about the metal detector," he told me.

"What did she say?"

"Nothing."

"Nothing?"

"Well . . . she laughed."

I was silent.

Cam continued. "We might be going to the beach tomorrow, so I thought I'd ask her for you."

"Thanks," I said sullenly.

"But she just laughed."

"I know. You told me that already."

Cam was silent for a few seconds. I waited for him to say something more, but he didn't.

"How's the bike riding going?" I finally asked him.

"Ummm . . . we're not really doing that anymore."

"How come?"

"Because Susie knocked my bike over and slugged me." I suddenly had visions of Charlotte's volleyball arm whacking me on the back and leaving me breathless. It gave me new respect for Susie the dog-dragger.

"Why did Susie do that?" I asked carefully.

"Oh, I told her that her dolls were dumb. Real babies are a lot better."

"That wasn't very nice, Cam," I said.

"No. But it was true." Cam paused for a moment. "Now Susie won't even talk to me."

I could certainly understand how Cam felt about that. Bobby and Charlotte had both been avoiding me like I had some strange tropical disease.

"You know what, Les?" Cam said, his voice squeaking over the telephone.

"What?"

"Girls are really different."

"That's for sure."

"You never know what they're thinking."

"That's for sure."

"Or what they're going to do next."

"That's for sure."

"Girls are just . . . weird."

Then Cam hung up.

11

For the next two days we did offense and defense drills. That was complicated, because it involved teamwork. You really had to anticipate what all of your opponents were going to do—not just one or two of them. And you had to work together with the guys on your own team, or else the entire strategy fell to pieces.

This morning Jake and I were on the same side, along with Terry and Jason Fuller, a tall blonde kid who roomed with Steve. Bobby and Tim were on Joe Minelli's team, and they were working on a "press" defense. Their team would rush us each time we tried to get under the basket, which forced us to take long shots.

It was difficult for any of us to drive our way in for a good lay-up, so I passed off to Jake and worked my way over to the corner of the court. But Jake lost ground and was surrounded.

"Here, Jake!" I yelled. He was oblivious. Aiming from the backcourt, he took a wild shot. It bounced off the backboard, and a guy named Scott retrieved it.

"SHREEEK!" Coach White ran onto the court, shaking his finger at Jake. "Crane was open, Lambert. Didn't you even see him?"

"Jake doesn't see anybody but Jake," someone muttered. I nodded angrily. I could have had that two points and Jake gave them away.

"Les was covered," Jake said defiantly. "Besides, I could have made that shot, no problem . . . if Les had been covering Scott."

Coach White snorted. "You're not the only kid at this camp, Lambert," he said. "You can either play on the team or go sit on the bench by yourself."

Jake smiled crookedly at him.

Then the coach realized that all of us were still standing there. "Let's break for lunch," he ordered.

I watched Coach White charge out the door, his open jacket flapping out on both sides. And I don't know who was angrier, him or me.

"What's the matter with you, Jake?" I cried. "I was wide open! Why did you have to go and hog the ball like that?"

Jake narrowed his eyes at me. "You would have missed that shot anyway, Les. And we all know it."

I was so mad at Jake that I felt like hitting him. But Tim put a hand on my shoulder, and I caught myself.

"I could have sunk that shot easily!" I shouted back at him.

Jake laughed and put an arm around me. "You want to use my ball. Right, little buddy?" he asked me. "Well, you can still have it. Just come with me on Thursday night."

The movie! With Charlotte! I still hadn't gotten close enough to apologize to her yet, but I wasn't sure I even wanted to. *The Return of Zorg* was only two days away now!

"Uh—Jake—" I began.

"Be there, Ichabod," Jake said, using that nickname I detested. Then he gave me a slap on the back and took off in the direction of the cafeteria.

"I wish that guy would just fall into a big hole," Steve said, shaking his head.

"Yeah. The same one he crawled out of," Terry added.

I was late to dinner that night, and by the time I got there, only the lasagne was left. It was cracked and dry, with reddish-black crusty stuff around the edges. I dished a piece out onto my plate and then stared at it uneasily.

"It tastes even worse than it looks, kid," remarked a voice behind me.

Charlotte! I was alone with her. Unprotected! But here was my chance. Immediately, I looked around for any signs of Charlotte's little bodyguard.

"Where's Bobby?" I asked.

"Over there. Talking to Jake."

I glanced quickly in the direction Charlotte was pointing, and at that very moment Jake caught sight of me in line with her.

"Hey, Leslie! Having dinner with your girlfriend?" he hooted loudly. I could hear a couple of guys at the other tables snickering.

"She's NOT my girlfriend!" I protested, slamming my tray back down. I glanced up at Charlotte, and her face sort of went stiff.

Cripes! Now I didn't know what to say to her. So I just headed out the door in a hurry, without looking back.

I walked quickly across the lawn and ran up the steps of our dorm building, two at a time. It wasn't until I got back to our room that I realized I had missed my big chance to apologize to Charlotte. And I had insulted her instead. All because of Jake.

Darn him anyway! Now I was in even more trouble with Charlotte. And he had made me miss dinner besides!

As I stared grimly at the crack in the ceiling I came to a decision. Jake had gone too far, and he had to be stopped! I would go to that movie on Thursday. Not because Jake had asked me to, but because I could apologize to Charlotte once and for all.

I would ask her for mercy, even if I had to kneel and beg. Then I would get that magic ball from Jake and stuff it down his grinning little throat!

There was a knock on the door, and Waldo let himself in.

"Your brother's on the phone again, Leslie," he said. Then he saw me sitting on the bed, my head between my hands. "Are you all right?"

"No," I answered gloomily.

"Want to talk about it?" His eyes looked huge behind those thick lenses.

"No, Waldo," I said, getting up. "But thanks anyway."

I answered the phone in the hall.

"Hi, Les. It's me."

"I know."

"How did you know?"

"Because you're the only one who ever calls me."

"Oh."

"What do you want?"

"Well, I just called to tell you that Susie and I made up."

I'll be darned. Maybe there was hope for me too.

"That's nice," I said.

"So, I'll be needing your bike again," Cam added.

I could feel myself getting angry. "Is that all?" I snapped.

"Uh, no. There's more." That figured. "We went to the beach, like I told you."

"So?"

"So there was a guy there with a metal detector. And I asked him how much it would cost me to get one."

"What did he say?"

"He said, 'More than you got, kid.'"

I laughed. "He was right, Cam."

"Well . . . maybe. But then I found forty-five cents on my own. In the parking lot."

"What did you do with it?"

"I showed it to the guy with the metal detector and told him I didn't need one after all."

That really made me laugh. I chuckled all the way back to my room. In fact, I even forgot about *The Return of Zorg*—for a while.

12

When I got to the auditorium on Thursday night Jake was already there, lingering near the entrance. I caught a glimpse of Bobby and Charlotte just inside the door. They were studying a full-length poster of Zorg.

"Why aren't you with them?" I asked Jake, pointing at the girls' backs.

"Well, uh, they don't exactly know that we're going to join them."

"WHAT?"

"Shhhh!" Jake peered over his shoulder and then leaned toward me. "I was waiting for you. I thought we could surprise them."

"Oh." We'd surprise them, all right. Slowly, we approached the two of them.

"Gross!" I heard Bobby squeal as she examined Zorg's two heads and four bulging eyes.

"Disgusting!" Charlotte agreed.

"Positively putrid!" Jake added over Bobby's right shoulder. She turned the other way and came face-to-face with me.

"Les!" she yelped. I started to speak, but Jake butted in.

"We came to see Zorg eat up New York, didn't we, Les?" he said.

I shrugged and then smiled shyly at Bobby and Charlotte. "I think he ate all of New York in the last movie," I remarked, but neither of them laughed. "Would you two like some popcorn?"

Bobby started to shake her head no.

"Yes, we would," Charlotte said suddenly, poking Bobby's arm. She stood up a little straighter, her head erect. "With lots of butter on it," she added.

"Okay. Lots of butter," Jake repeated with his lopsided grin. Then he bugged his eyes out just like Zorg. Bobby giggled, but I could only watch Jake in disgust as he strolled over to the snack table. What did she find so humorous about that baboon?

The girls started down the aisle ahead of Jake and me. Jake was carrying two big tubs of buttered popcorn. He handed one of them to me.

"I think they're going to sit with us," Jake whispered.

"What will we talk about?" I whispered back. I

tried to think of some acceptable subjects, but my mind drew a blank. Every time I spoke to Charlotte, horrible things seemed to come out.

Glancing nervously at Charlotte, I hoped Jake wouldn't say anything that would get us in trouble. I thought about his dumb jokes and decided to steer him away from further danger. "Just remember, your Charlotte 'MASS' jokes are taboo."

We walked down the aisle to look for four empty seats. As Bobby started down a row Jake jumped in after her, pulling me with him. Charlotte just shrugged and followed.

When we were seated I handed Charlotte the tub of popcorn and then Jake whispered loudly in my ear, "What's 'taboo'?"

"It means 'off limits,'" I told him. "'Don't touch.'"

"What do you mean 'Don't touch'?" Charlotte protested. "You just handed me the popcorn!" She leaned her body toward mine, and I closed my eyes, taking a deep breath.

"Mind if I lean this way, kid?" she asked me. "I can't see over that girl's hairdo." Charlotte pointed to the person in front of us. The girl's hair really was hideous. Piled up on top of her head like that, it looked like a knitted tornado.

I smiled weakly at Charlotte and nodded. The lights started to dim, and she dug into the popcorn. That's when it hit me. Charlotte Nass was actually talking to me. Sort of. At least she hadn't inflicted any bodily injuries. And she hadn't yelled at me either. Jeez! Sitting next to her really hadn't been so hard after all. I relaxed a little and began watching the show.

When Zorg came on the screen Jake started making throw-up noises and Charlotte screamed. Half of her popcorn fell on my lap, but I wasn't about to say anything.

Old Tornado-Head turned around and whispered "Shhh!"

It was really too dark to get a good look at her face, but Jake said, "Man! She has both of Zorg's heads beat, hands down!" He laughed and made a very loud noise with one hand in his armpit. You know the kind I mean.

Bobby giggled, but I heard her whisper "Stop it!"

About halfway through the movie Jake tried to put his arm around Bobby. Or at least I think he did. Because I could hear him rustling around beside me, and then Bobby whispering something like, "Hands off, Jake!"

I know he heard that, because he suddenly leaned over in my direction, jerking his elbow up at the same time, and he jabbed me right in the stomach.

"For cryin' out loud, Jake. Will you cut that out?" I yelled.

Tornado-Head whipped around again. "Shhhh!" she ordered. I scrunched down in my seat, but I noticed that Jake's other hand was back in his lap.

Finally, the handsome star of the movie rescued the girl and sent Zorg running (leaving the possibility open for a Zorg III movie, no doubt). Jake made smooching noises as the actors kissed, and then Tornado-Head turned around to really glare at us.

When the lights came on, all four of us walked into the lobby together. Bobby immediately headed for the door, and Charlotte handed me the empty tub.

"Thanks for the popcorn, kid," Charlotte said, jutting her chin out at me. She turned to follow Bobby.

"Sure," I answered vaguely. But I suddenly realized that this was my chance. I could apologize to Charlotte right now. Gathering up all of my courage, I opened my mouth.

"Charlotte," I began, "I—I—" But by this time, all I could see of Charlotte was her back, already halfway through the auditorium door.

I set off after her, running down the auditorium steps. I could just see her at the bottom of the stairs when Jake caught up to me from behind.

"The deal is off, Les!" he shouted, loud enough for Charlotte to hear him. "Bobby didn't say a word to me after the movie. She just split!

So I really don't think you should get my basketball just for sitting next to Charlotte—"

Charlotte came to a halt. Then she whipped around and charged up the stairs to us.

"Jake, you're just a conceited creep!" she shouted. Then she paused and peered at me. This is it, I thought. Go ahead and pound me!

"I thought that maybe this was your weird little way of saying you were sorry, kid. Bobby told me that you really are a nice guy, but I guess she was wrong."

Bobby said that? I was too stunned to answer.

It didn't matter. Charlotte just left me there anyway. I watched her hasty retreat down the steps.

And suddenly I had a strange empty feeling. Like Charlotte had actually pulled something out of my insides or something. By this time, I should have been used to girls running away from me in anger. After all, this was getting to be a pretty routine event in my life.

But knowing that didn't make it hurt any less. Right now, I felt like the lowest form of pond scum.

Without a word to Jake I headed back to our room. I could hear him following behind me, but I wouldn't slow down. I was furious with him!

I stopped right in front of the dorm steps. Two girls were sitting there, sharing a candy bar. Girls!

Cam was right. They just messed everything up!

Then I heard Jake running up behind me. "Hey, watch out, ladies!" he yelled with a laugh. "That guy is an axe murderer!"

One girl screamed. I turned around in a daze. This was it. The last straw. Something inside my head just went . . . ping! All I knew was that Jake had made Charlotte hate me and Bobby hate me. And now I even hated myself too!

"You TURKEY!" I screamed at Jake, pouncing on him and knocking him down on his back.

I had never fought with anyone in my life before, but I don't think either one of us really knew the finer points of wrestling. We just sort of squirmed around on the ground, like two pigs wiggling their way out of a sack. One of the girls was yelling, "Oh, gross! Look—blood!"

I rolled off Jake and stared up at the stars in the sky. Bleeding? Oh, Gawd!!! What had that maniac done to me? I reached one hand up to feel my nose for blood. But it was dry as a sand dune.

I heard Jake get up and sniffle a few times. It took me a minute to figure out what he was doing. Then all of a sudden it hit me. Jake Lambert was crying! I looked up and caught a glimpse of his face under the lamp in front of the dorm.

Blood was dripping out of one of his nostrils. And Jake was wiping an arm across his eyes and

101

under his nose. His T-shirt was all stained from the grass and dirt we had been wiggling around in. And there might even have been some blood on it too. I couldn't really tell in the dark.

Jake turned away slowly and made his way around the screaming girls and up the stairs, but I didn't move. I could feel that my right hand was throbbing now. I wiggled my fingers and balled them up into a fist. Then I looked at it. Somehow or another, that fist had managed to make contact with Jake's nose.

I was still lying on my back when Waldo's head suddenly appeared above mine. I guess he had run out of the dorm and down the steps the minute he found out what had happened.

"Are you okay, Crane?" he asked cautiously.

"Yeah," I answered. Then I smiled slyly. "I'm feeling just great."

As Waldo helped me up to my feet, I rubbed my tingling fingers together and realized that I had never felt better in my life. Really.

"I'd better go find Jake," Waldo said. "Why don't you get yourself cleaned up?" He patted my shoulder and marched up the steps quickly before turning around at the top. "Are you sure you're all right?"

I nodded and followed him into the dorm. Jake was not in our room. Not that I really expected him to be. But Tim was sitting on his bed, scribbling on the back of a postcard.

"What did you do to Jake?" he asked, looking up at me.

"He looked pretty bad, huh?"

"Like a dying buffalo."

I tried to hold back a grin. "I really didn't mean to hit him," I explained. "It was an accident."

"I think it was an accident waiting to happen," Tim answered.

Later, as I was lying in bed, Waldo came in and said he would have to call my parents about this in the morning. Waldo also informed us that Jake would be staying in another room for the remaining two nights of camp.

I felt sorry for Waldo. This was probably not in any of his big books full of graphs and hieroglyphics. But I had to hand it to him: Waldo had remained totally calm.

I realized that Mom and Dad were going to be very angry and disappointed in me. And thinking about them suddenly made me feel sad and homesick. I closed my eyes, fighting back warm tears. Finally, I rolled over onto my stomach and thumped my pillow.

"Les?" Tim whispered after Waldo was gone.

"Mmmm?"

"I sure wish I had done that."

I smiled slowly in the darkness and wiped my nose. Then I even laughed softly. Tim couldn't have cheered me up any faster. Not even if he had just told me I was the best ball player in the whole state.

13

Friday was our exhibition game. All of the different sports groups at camp would be giving demonstrations, but basketball was the first one scheduled.

Right after breakfast we headed for the courts. And the word was out. Coach White was going to let us play with the "magic" ball. Jake would finally have his lucky charm back, but would it really work?

Kids from the other parts of camp gathered around to watch too, especially after they learned that we would be using Jake's ball.

Scanning the bleachers, I caught a glimpse of Charlotte, sitting up very straight and watching the players run through their drills. I figured she was either there to cheer Bobby on or to put a hex on me. Then I noticed Waldo sitting calmly about three rows up. Waldo?

He caught my eye and waved. Then he even gave me a thumbs-up. I smiled back and gave him a thumbs-up too. Let's face it. If he had told Coach White about my fight with Jake last night, I might already be on my way home.

The coach blew his whistle, and we took our places on the court. Tim and Jake were the two centers. My job was to cover Jake.

Within a minute of play Jake had fired the ball up twice, sinking it both times. I was guarding him so closely that I could see three tiny beads of sweat resting right over his upper lip.

"Two buckets to nothing!" he shouted happily, doing that wild little dance with his feet. Then he stopped directly in front of me, and his smile froze. I stared back at him without blinking, and I wondered if he was going to say anything about the fight. But the whistle blew, and Jake was the first one to look away. He turned his back to me, and I walked over to the bench for a time-out.

Tim threw an arm around my shoulders. "Stop concentrating on Jake so much and just keep your eye on the ball," he advised me.

I nodded stupidly. What was the difference, anyway, I complained to myself. Jake seemed unbeatable.

The horn sounded, and I walked out onto the

court with Tim. Heeding his advice, I tried to mentally block Jake from my vision by staring at the orange ball cradled under his palm. I could see the "Magic" signature bouncing up and down as Jake dribbled. And I wanted to know what that ball felt like. Hardly anyone had been able to get his hands on it yet.

Jake head-faked to the left. I paid no attention to his head. The ball, I told myself, the ball. Just watch the ball. Then Jake began to work his way to the right from the top of the key. He dribbled the ball forward, but I wouldn't let him through to the hoop. I was on him, and I could tell that he was starting to get rattled because his eyes were darting back and forth. I think Jake was just too proud to pass the ball off, so he jumped, lofting it over my head toward the basket.

He totally overshot, and that was just the chance I needed. As the ball teetered off the edge of the hoop, I grabbed it and sped down the court like lightning. Jake was the only one after me, but by the time I crossed the center line, I was alone. This was it! My chance! I sped on to the basket, certain that I couldn't miss.

At the same time, a yell rose from the stands. Jake was on me! Without stopping to think, I leaped into the air and banked the ball in off the backboard. A perfect shot!

What happened after that is kind of hard to ex-

plain. I guess it was like the whole world sort of slackened its pace, but I didn't. And it felt as if everything was moving in slow motion while I just stood there watching.

It took Jake a few moments to realize what I had done. Or, actually, what he had done. Jake Lambert had missed a shot back there. That was all. But for one instant I saw his face collapse, and I almost regretted recovering the ball at all.

Personally, I didn't even care about that dumb ball. And I don't think Jake did either. Not really. But he had told everyone so much about it and made such a big deal out of how good he was that maybe he did believe in it. Just a little. And now he had gone and missed an easy shot, by a mile.

While I was watching his face, I still held the "magic" ball in my hands. I could feel every bump and line on its surface, and yet all of this had taken place in less than a minute. It was like running a videotape on slow speed.

The stands were eerily silent. All of my teammates on the court were quiet. I think everyone except the coach had somehow heard about my fight with Jake last night, and they were waiting to see what Jake would do now. Then I heard a single voice call out to me loud and clear from the bleachers:

"Good rebound, kid."

It was Charlotte.

I looked up at her and blinked once. Then the stands erupted into yells and cheers, and I slowly let myself smile back at her.

Jake yanked the ball out of my hands and charged off the court, not saying a word to anyone. The entire crowd watched him storm out of the gym.

When I looked over at Coach White, he just shook his head slowly back and forth. He threw another ball to me and motioned for us to keep on playing. I guess the exhibition game was going to continue, even if we had to play one man short.

Waldo was waiting for me when I walked into the dorm later that afternoon.

"I want to talk to you, Crane," he said.

"Is this about my fight with Jake?" I asked quietly, ready for the worst. "Did you call my dad?"

"No," answered Waldo, shoving his glasses up on his nose. "I haven't called your father yet."

"Why not?"

"I thought that maybe I would wait and call him after you got home."

I didn't say anything, but I considered dropping to my knees and begging.

"But maybe I won't tell him anything about it," Waldo continued very slowly. "What you did to Jake today was far worse than a punch in the nose anyway."

"I didn't do anything to Jake today!" I shouted, suddenly angry at him. "Jake just missed a shot. We've all done that."

"But you took the ball away from him," Waldo reminded me. "And you made the shot. With everyone in the entire camp watching."

I hadn't thought of it like that, but Waldo was probably right. Even though I had given Jake a bloody nose last night, he was still king of the basketball courts . . . until today.

"Where is Jake now?" I asked, looking around.

"Gone."

"Gone where?"

"I gave him a pass. His parents are going to drive here and pick him up this afternoon."

"Oh." I suddenly felt sorry for Jake, and a little guilty. And I guess my face must have shown it.

"Hey, it wasn't your fault," Waldo said, awkwardly patting me on the back. "You played well today."

"Thanks."

I started off to my room, but then I just had to know something, so I turned around. "What are you studying to be, anyway, Waldo?" I asked him.

"A doctor," he answered proudly.

I thought about that. Waldo probably wasn't much of a basketball player, but he might actually be a good doctor someday. At least I was pretty sure he wouldn't end up on the beach with a metal detector.

"Well, good luck," I replied, and I really meant it.

As I passed the phone in the hall, I noticed the mail lying in a heap on the table. Right on top was a letter addressed to me. I ripped it open and began reading:

Dear Les,

We all miss you, so it will be nice to see you on Saturday. However, I have some bad news for you. Your bike is ruined.

Cam took it and started to ride down Sand Hill at top speed. I tried to stop him, but he got pedaling much too fast. I kept yelling at him to bail out, but he hung on for dear life and finally landed in a heap at the bottom of the hill. He's fine, but the bike's a wreck.

I am very sorry about this, but I will buy you a new bicycle as soon as the next Cadillac drives off my lot.

Lots of love,
                                        Dad

112

He told Cam to bail out! Bail out! That was my bike Dad was talking about, lying in a gutter somewhere. And if I had been there, this never would have happened in the first place!

Well, I didn't care now if Cam ever learned to ride a bicycle. He could just push Susie Walker's dolls around Riverdale for the rest of his life, for all I cared.

And after this, if Cam thought he was getting that thirteen dollars from me, he was crazy!

14

The cafeteria was thinly disguised as a dance hall that night for our farewell party. I hated dances. All the guys lined up on one side of the room and all the girls lined up on the other. Then, when we finally got up enough nerve to go out there and move our feet, we still lined ourselves up in two straight rows down the center of the room. I'm serious! It looked like we were dancing the Virginia reel or something.

Just for protection, I decided to plant my own feet near the punch bowl, when I felt that familiar volleyball arm thumping me between the shoulder blades.

"Hi, kid," Charlotte said. She poured herself a glass of punch and spilled some of it over the edge of the glass. Then she looked down at me

114

uncertainly. "That was a great shot you made this afternoon."

"Thanks."

Charlotte put her glass back down on the table. "I guess Jake is gone now, isn't he?"

My eyes narrowed. "How did you know about that?" I asked.

"Tim told me."

"Oh." I wondered if Tim had also told her how rotten I felt about everything that had happened.

I squinted up at her, wondering if she was still mad at me. And I decided that Charlotte didn't look angry. Not exactly. But she was frowning at me.

I realized that all this time I had wanted to apologize to Charlotte, I had never tried just talking to her. The truth of this sort of hit my brain like a sledgehammer. But there was another truth too, and I had to let it out.

"You know, Charlotte, I didn't like you at first," I admitted. And once I said it, I felt that emptiness inside of me starting to fill up. "I was scared of you," I said quietly, staring down at the floor, "but I'm not anymore. So I do like you now . . . I guess."

Then Charlotte did something that really took me by surprise. She smiled at me. A real genuine smile, with all her teeth showing. And, you know,

Charlotte had a really nice smile! She was still pretty tall, but that was okay.

"Would you like to dance?" she asked me all of a sudden. I wanted desperately to say no, but I was too afraid of hurting her feelings again, now that she seemed to be on speaking terms with me. So she and I joined the Virginia reel.

As soon as the song was over I backstepped and tried to execute a quick exit.

"Hold it, Les," Charlotte said, grabbing my arm. "I know you just danced with me on the rebound—" I made a funny face at her, and she suddenly realized what an awful pun she had just made.

Charlotte thumped me on the back again and laughed. I even laughed too. I couldn't believe it. I was actually laughing with Charlotte Nass!

"What I meant," Charlotte continued to say, "was that Bobby is the one you really like, and you should be dancing with her."

"In case you haven't noticed," I snapped sarcastically, "Bobby isn't even talking to me."

"Oh, she's just giving you a little of your own medicine," Charlotte replied.

"Huh?"

"You haven't talked to her either, you know."

This was humbling. I suddenly felt like a fool.

Charlotte laughed again, and I realized that I had a chance now to finally apologize to her.

"Look, Charlotte," I blurted out, "I'm sorry about the score cards. Really! And my mean crack in the cafeteria. It was all Jake's idea anyway, and—"

"Oh, Jake!" scoffed Charlotte, angrily. "He's a potato head."

Where had I heard that before?

Then Charlotte looked seriously at me, the corners of her mouth turned down in a frown. "That stunt you guys pulled with the score cards was pretty mean, you know? I hated you and Jake. A lot."

"But do you hate me now? I mean, still?" I asked, smiling up at her in bright desperation.

"No. You're a pretty good kid," she said, patting me on the shoulder. Cripes! She did it again—called me a kid. "Tim thinks so too," she added.

"Tim?" I said. What did he have to do with this?

"Well, I—uh—I mean Tim—" Charlotte looked down at her hands for a moment. Then she suddenly tightened her jaw and aimed a look at me down her nose. "Well, never mind, kid."

Charlotte was actually blushing! Then I remembered where I had heard "potato head" before.

Tim was making his way over to the punch bowl, and Charlotte began to giggle nervously. Jeez! I wasn't so sure I ever wanted to turn thir-

117

teen, if that's how people got. I, for one, would never call an eleven-year-old boy "kid." And I certainly wouldn't giggle like that!

With a shrug of my shoulders I trotted off to find Bobby and make my last apology for a while. I finally spotted her across the room dancing with Waldo, and they made quite a pair. Bobby was twirling around the floor on her tiptoes and Waldo was just standing in one place, moving his head up and down in time to the music.

When they were finished dancing, Waldo left and I shuffled up to Bobby, trying to look as pathetically sorry as I could.

"I'm sorry, Bobby," I mumbled.

Bobby giggled. "Oh, for goodness' sake, Les," she laughed. "You look like a sick dog."

"You mean you're not mad at me anymore?"

"Of course I am!" she said. "But I was just waiting for you to apologize. That's all."

I sighed. Girls really were too weird to even begin to figure out.

"And you don't like Jake?" I inquired.

"Jake? Oh, he's a great basketball player. And I thought he was kind of funny. But I never LIKED him. He's a total jerk. And a bully! And a potato head."

"Do you want to dance?" I asked her suddenly. I couldn't believe I was actually saying that.

"Sure," she answered. Then she crinkled up her nose at me, and I got that dizzy, gray numb feeling all over again.

Dad was there to pick me up at school when the bus pulled in the next morning. I told him all about my two weeks at camp, and I even confessed to brawling on the ground with Jake. Dad didn't seem too surprised, though, so I figured Waldo had phoned him after all.

"But I think that you had better call that boy tomorrow and apologize to him," my father insisted, his hands firmly gripping the steering wheel.

Oh, no! Not another apology! I whipped down the window on my side of the car and screamed loudly at the cars in the lane next to us. Then I calmly rolled the window back up.

When I turned to face my father, he was staring in horror at me.

"It's okay, Dad," I assured him. "I'll do it, but I don't have to like doing it."

When we pulled into the garage, the first thing I wanted to do was to get a good look at my injured bicycle. I jumped out of the car immediately and started looking for it. But my bike was gone! In its place stood a brand new ten-speed bike with French racing tires.

119

As soon as I saw that bike, I wasn't angry at Cam anymore. I just rubbed my hands over the hard leather seat and the rounded handlebars. Then I spun one of the pedals around with the toe of my sneaker. I couldn't wait to call Mike and describe the entire bicycle to him in detail.

The contents of my duffel bag were already strewn all over my bed by the time Cam walked into our room.

He carefully pulled a wad of paper towel out of his pocket. Then he unwrapped it in front of me.

I stared at the tooth that was inside.

"It's my third one, but I'm not going to tell Dad this time," Cam whispered.

I looked down at him and smiled slyly. "Remember what I told you," I said. "Twelve more years and that thing'll be worth pure gold."

Then I handed him thirteen dollars.

After dinner I offered to help Mom wash the dishes. Even stacking up those same old glasses and salad bowls made me feel good. It was just so nice to be in my own kitchen again, with all those familiar smells, that I didn't really want to leave the room yet.

"It sure is good having you home again, Les," Mom said suddenly, giving me a big wet kiss. I made a face, but I hugged her back.

Just then Cam trudged solemnly into the kitchen, clutching his photograph of Susie. He proceeded to tear up the picture in front of our very eyes.

"Mom, can you burn this?" he asked her.

"Why?"

"Because Susie's grandmother told me that when Susie went to the day-care center she cried. But by the time her mom came to pick her up, Susie was happy again because she had two new boyfriends already."

"Oh," Mom replied, taking the torn-up photograph from him. "Well, we don't keep matches in the house. Why don't I just put Susie into the trash compactor instead?"

"Okay." Then Cam watched in silence as the compactor groaned and buzzed for a few minutes. When it was all over, Cam turned and walked slowly away.

"Does this mean the wedding is off?" Mom yelled after him.

I couldn't blame .Cam in some ways, though. Girls were sure a pain sometimes. I ran after him.

Halfway down the hall, I caught up with my brother and placed a hand sympathetically on his shoulder. I did feel sorry for him. But I couldn't help smiling to myself.

After all, I was going bicycle riding tomorrow with Mike and Bobby. I couldn't wait to show both of them my new bike. And I might even give them a head start at the top of the hill.

Then, just when they thought they had left me in the dust, I would blow right by them with those fancy French racing tires. There I'd be, Leslie Crane. Laughing my head off all the way down Sand Hill Drive.